ZACHARY JEFFRIES

Angel of Fate

ANGEL OF FATE

ZACHARY JEFFRIES

Author's Note

Dear Reader,

Please don't keep this book a secret! Feel free to let your friends, family, loved ones, and strangers know what you're reading. Post about it on social media. Spread the word to your bookish friends! Each of books is an investment of hundreds of hours and thousands of dollars. Every moment you can spare helping this book find the right readers is appreciated more than you know.

Sincerely,

-Z

Dedication

For my love.

I'm happy to be your over-dramatic brooding partner because you are a badass force-of-nature with unknowable potential.

Reader, Be Aware

This book includes:

Anxiety

Death, including death of immediate family

Mental Illness

Occult

Involuntary commitment to mental facility

Suicidal thoughts

Physical violence

Chapter 1

Cain

Whether or not he physically existed, Cain couldn't shake the sinking feeling. He stood on the curb right next to where the car accident was going to take place. Waiting. Restless. Focused. Prepared, but not ready.

After shifting to human to check his phone for the third time that minute, Cain settled back into his Reaper form before any passing cars could see him. His bony body was still, a perfect human skeleton now topped with white deer antlers. What had been thick rolls of a black robe was now dangling tatters. Cain felt he looked especially Pagan-couture, rustic but fashionable, which gave him a sense of confidence. With how jumbled and unpredictable his Reaper forms were, it was nice to have a cohesive look, even if no one could see.

He looked at his own reflection in the shops of downtown South Aurora, streets lit in yellow populated by random cars on the way home from bars. His pale, skeletal figure crouched with his head slightly tilted gave the most menacing look, Cain decided.

The screech and the crash came one after the other, noise on top of noise. Noise before Cain identified the action. A blue compact sports car wrapped around a lamppost. Cain hadn't seen it coming, and then it was over. Now the car was stopped, ticking and smoking.

The soul!

Cain searched the wreckage, peering through smoke he couldn't swat away in the otherworldliness of his Reaper form. He really hoped the person wasn't suffering. Not that Cain had any affection for the souls he culled, or any mere human for that matter... Not that he'd ever officially culled a soul entirely on his own before, either.

And so he searched, scared to look further as he found streaks of blood. He didn't want to see a mess is what he told himself, flinching as he followed the blood trail up to the burst windshield. He listened for whimpering. Silence.

Through the smoke, past the car, he saw more blood leading to a crumpled pile of clothing, likely full of person. A person who might have been suffering. A person Cain had to release from suffering and from their earthbound physical form.

He approached slowly, carefully, knowing full well those closest to crossing over had the best chance to perceive a Reaper, to glimpse Death as they met. On the nearby sidewalk, the person, or the body, was perfectly still, clothes dark under the yellow light, one gloved hand sticking out. No, not gloved. Bloody.

The sight gave Cain pause. Moments passed. Maybe minutes.

The car exploded. Right behind Cain. He leapt forward and tumbled. He wasn't thrown by the blast or hurt by the fire in this form, but the sound and force startled him.

It wasn't like a car exploding in the movies. Reality was just smoke and a din, then a car laid out as if infirmed. Cain caught his breath although he wasn't breathing, convincing himself he was safe.

The soul!

The rumpled pile was moving clearly, rhythmically. Breathing? Gasping? Coughing?

Cain approached carefully still, though he knew time was fleeting. He hated himself for his uncertainty, hated the fear within him. This was the disgusting humanity his parents forced on him. A Reaper shouldn't hesitate.

The body was curled up, gasping, shaking. Dying. Cain just had to put him out of his misery, but the image slowed him. This person on the ground was shivering in pain, afraid, vulnerable. It was all too intimate, too exposed. Cain didn't want to harvest the soul, couldn't bring himself to feel those awful feelings of the dying man. He just couldn't convince himself to cull the soul.

Then the darkness came. It sounded like the hush of curtains being drawn. It chilled the blood while heating the skin, and Cain was grateful he was ethereal at that moment. The darkness swept along the street, dimming yellow streetlights and bringing freezing wind.

Father.

No, no, no. Cain had to act fast. He could do this, he had to. This was Cain's assigned soul on the ground, looking straight into Cain's shaded bony eye sockets. Cain reached his bleached finger out to grasp at the soul...

Quickly, the darkness of Death passed over them, through them. The crash victim gasped as his face contorted into seizing, crying horror, and then he relaxed entirely as his soul left. Cain was too late. His hesitation had cost him the assignment.

And Father continued down the cobblestone street, dimming lights and whipping stray garbage into a frenzy.

Then the normal world reset the way it always did after a supernatural being of great power exited. The early spring air warmed again, and the crash victim was no longer a person but a cadaver on the sidewalk.

Cain had failed. Again.

Time was running out to prove that he could do this, to drop the part-time human routine. A failure like this didn't help. Cain was furious with himself.

With a heavy sigh, Cain fell back onto his heels into his pale, fleshy yet thin human form. He took a minute before getting up and beginning the long walk home. He couldn't walk to Lockport from here in one night. He'd have to eventually shift forms again, but for that moment, he needed the time alone. And none of his other forms could shout curse words or cry.

The next car Cain encountered, he actually heard approaching. The familiar hum of his mom's sedan crept behind him as the window went down.

"C'mon, I'll give you a ride," Mom said.

Cain didn't put up a fight and got in. "How'd you get here so quick?"

"Your father and I were out."

"I interrupted date night?" Cain felt even worse. His parents' schedules rarely lined up, so a date night was a big deal.

"Oh come on, Cain, you didn't interrupt anything. Our lives interrupt your father's work."

"Was he mad?"

"Mad? What? At you? Are you kidding me? Cain, he's worried, not mad."

His dad was worried about him? That softened Cain a bit. Father wasn't exactly warm or affectionate, but at least he was on Cain's side if he was worried about his son...

"You're at an age, Cain, when you're finding out a lot of the stuff that you believe in to be true, to be rock solid, to be eternal, just...isn't."

"What, like Santa Claus? Or the United States?" Cain sneered at his own joke.

"Like Death."

That got Cain's attention.

His mom continued, "I know your father is good at what he does-"

Cain scoffed, "He's perfect."

"But just because you haven't seen him fail, Cain, doesn't mean he can't. Our way of Death—culling souls, guiding them to pass over—is not guaranteed."

Looking out the window at the evergreens and budding trees lining the freeway, he played it off. "What are you talking about, Mom? Death is the only thing guaranteed besides taxes."

"Well, let me put it this way. You know how the sun rises in the East and sets in the West?"

"Yes?"

"Always, right?"

"Yeah."

"Well, Cain, if you do become a Reaper and do become immortal, you'll live to see a time when the Earth crashes into the Sun."

"So when there are no more people, there will be no death?"

"That's not what I'm saying, Cain. I'm saying what we do, what your father does...it's a fragile thing. It can get taken away. Nothing lasts forever. Not taxes. Not Death. Something could come along and really throw a wrench in the machinery. And that keeps your father up at night. Well, when he manages to sleep. We're your parents, and we're always going to worry about you, but... Cain, this is Death. A basic element in the balance of the universe. And we are worried that you are just not ready to wield it."

They sat in silence for the rest of the ride home.

Chapter 2

MaKayla

MaKayla rushed into the sanctuary of her room. Surrounded by the walls of her collage art, she closed the door behind her and took a breath. She left the outside world behind her, all the stress from her school day, her fender-bender in the parking lot, her shouting match with Ivy Skelton. With another deep breath, she forgave herself for getting caught up in her own anxiety.

But there was still the mystery of this box.

She'd done her best to inconspicuously check her car bumpers for scratches before she walked into the house, but then she hit an obstacle. Or the front door did. A package. A medium-sized rectangle, smaller than a shoe box, bigger than a sunglasses case.

Now, if anyone was a sucker for well-wrapped packages, it was MaKayla. The intricately decorated empty jewelry boxes on her bookshelf made that obvious. But after getting a closer look at the box in the mail, MaKayla wasn't too impressed. Longer than it was wide, the package was coated in mismatched postage stamps and stickers—Germany, Russia, Fragile, Careful: Sharp Objects, American Customs, official police business, warnings in German.

And MaKayla's name and address. Her full name, including the embarrassing middle name she never told anyone, much less someone from Germany. And on the return address label was another: Elena Corinthia.

MaKayla's dead grandmother, her mom's late estranged mom. The Greek source of MaKayla's brown and olive tones that differed from her otherwise WASPy family. The puzzle coming together horrified and confused MaKayla. Was her grandmother *not* dead?

She gasped. She'd never read her grandmother's name before; her mother had removed all traces of it. Mom would legit spit on the floor if anyone even mentioned the deceased woman. "Died long before you were born, and she can't hurt us now," was all she'd ever say for as long as MaKayla could remember. From what she had pried out of her dad, MaKayla knew her grandmother passed away in a Russian asylum that got too cold in the winter. It was a story that had always broken MaKayla's heart. How scared the woman must have been, how sad and alone.

If any of that was true.

And now, from this ugly little box, the woman's name was staring impossibly up at MaKayla, glaring at her, a name that somehow was coercing MaKayla to conspire against Mom.

Because there was no doubt that Mom would be against MaKayla's opening the package. Or any package from a supposed long-dead person, really, but especially one from Elena Corinthia (and now she was imagining Mom spitting on the floor).

It was most likely absolutely nothing. More junk mail, like a scam using a loved one's name. But then, why go to all the trouble of sending a package?

Outside, she heard her mom's car pulled up, and MaKayla found herself cradling the small box, rushing to open it. She ran her box cutter across the brown paper between stickers and stamps with a satisfyingly slick sound.

Once it was unwrapped, she couldn't believe the box. This couldn't be right. This package couldn't be for her.

It was very official-looking. "Evidence" was printed on the white cardboard, and other lines striped the box below, everything else censored with thick black marker, only showing peeks of different handwriting. Each redacted line had a date next to it, almost completely blacked out, but the tops of the numbers were visible enough to show decades passed between each line of writing.

Line after line on the evidence box had been redacted except a few. "Personal effect, ship to next-of-kin," then that haunted name once again, and the word "deceased" followed by last week's date.

Her grandmother had been locked away for years and years and years, and somehow had her last possessions shipped to the granddaughter she never met? Wasn't Mom her next-of-kin? The box brought up so many questions, but one thought solidified into certainty. and made MaKayla's stomach sink.

Mom lied. Her grandmother had died last week.

That box had taken a long ride just to stare up at MaKayla silently from her desk. She wasn't sure what to do. Opening it felt wrong, though not like a betrayal of her mother; MaKayla was way past that. It felt illegal. The box was clearly official police business.

Should MaKayla wear gloves to keep her prints off? Should she contact the local police? Ask an adult like Mom? Or wait and ask Dad, the parent less likely to have lied to her for her entire life?

Despite all that, she opened it anyway. Curiosity drove her to it, as well as the labeling of the box and a feeling that the contents now belonged to her. It was sent to her. On purpose. By a dead woman.

She cut the piece of tape tasked with containing secret evidence from the world. She slid the cardboard top open.

Within was an unassuming brown triangle, less than a foot long. Something was wrapped in brown paper and more tape, rather sloppily.

But wow, it was heavier than it seemed.

With her chipped pink nails, she picked at the edge of the tape until it stood up enough to pinch and peel away. She carefully unfolded each edge of the brown paper to reveal an old, tarnished pair of scissors.

Scissors? That was it?

She studied them for a moment, inspecting for bloodstains or hair or any other grisly reminder of violence, but found none. In fact, they were nice scissors, just a bit discolored. She snipped them open and shut easily, the blades slicing through the air. The little bolt holding the blades was still tight, and MaKayla wondered if they were still sharp.

Being as crafty as she was, MaKayla appreciated a good pair of scissors.

She grabbed a small length of lacy ribbon and gave it a snip. Nothing. The ribbon remained uncut. She tried again. Nothing. Again, and again, and again, she tried and could not penetrate the lace. Curious, but kind of annoying.

She tried a thin flat fabric ribbon, but nothing. Cheap plastic wrapping ribbon—nothing. Yarn—nope. What good were these things?

The scissors, though used, were new to her, and she didn't want to commit the cardinal sin of ruining the blades by cutting paper, but if they weren't sharp enough for ribbon, she would like to use them for *something*.

So, she picked up some construction paper and went to town, opening and closing, but the scissors left no mark. The blades didn't bite into the sheet. She ripped a piece of notebook paper, then a thick bookmark, a cheap paperback, a piece of thread, her own shirt, her own hair... She found scissors could slice none of them.

She did find, however, on the other side of the scissors, glinting up at her from the outside of the blade, an inscription, shiny gray in the tarnished black metal. Clearly and sharply, in perfect font, read MaKayla's full name.

Cain

Killing healthy people was, for the most part, a clean process. Cain had done it dozens of times...with his parents' help. Healthy people were just so much easier and less suspecting than the sick. Sick people clung to life actively, consciously holding onto that lifeline, while the healthy didn't think about it. They sauntered about confidently without a care in the world.

Cain understood; whenever he caught a cold, he thought to himself that he should appreciate his health more once he felt better. But he never did. Conversely, when he did think he was going to die (only once, when he got seasick), he too clung to life with all of his might.

Which was ridiculous, of course. A Reaper wouldn't die at only seventeen years old. His own parents were thousands of years old and still spry. But in his defense, seasickness is quite a to-do.

Every time he found himself staring into the family's eternal flame on a full moon for the identity of the next soul to take, he hoped the person was healthy.

Maybe that was in bad taste, that he preferred to strike someone down while they were brimming with zeal and life, but he enjoyed plucking ripe fruit.

So he was nervous coming home the night of the full moon.

It didn't help that the moment he walked in his house, before he could even drop his keys in the little bowl on the buffet, before he could take off his chunky black boots and line them up alongside this parents', Mom's superhuman voice thunderously proclaimed, "Tis a full moon tonight!"

"I know." He carefully unlaced his boots and stood them up next to her running shoes.

"Is there something you want to tell me about?" Mom came into the kitchen in her fleshy human form, but Cain didn't doubt that her visage matched her voice just moments ago.

"Not if I don't have to."

Mom was in yoga pants and a robe as usual, the maroon robe matching Cain's nails. Her wavy deep brown hair was perfect, as always. "Is this about school or staring into the eternal flame?"

"Maybe the flame a little."

"Well, just remember everything your father and I have taught you, and don't be afraid to ask us questions leading up to the culling."

"Easy for you to say. Your first years reaping were all Neanderthals."

"You're much too clever for such plebeian jokes. And besides, I earned my bones taking caveman souls." She winked at him.

If Mom was making jokes about her age, then she was nervous, too.

He tossed his backpack onto the giant pine kitchen table and dug out the books he needed for homework.

Mom made a smoothie for two but shifted gears once she handed the strawberry mango mixture to her son. She cringed as she asked, "Can we talk about what happened at school today?"

"No, not if I don't have to."

"Cain, I'm on a first name basis with your principal now."

"Great, so we all agree, I won't go back to school." He fished a copy of Wuthering Heights out of his backpack, climbed over his homework on the table and fit himself into one of the large wooden sills of the big old house.

"Please, Cain." Mom set to emptying the dishwasher. She always seemed too elegant doing housework. "Your father and I like it here. And you can believe me that having a home and blending in is much more sustainable than being a rampant, drifting spirit."

"You and Father always say that, but I've personally always identified as a rampant, drifting spirit."

"Really? There's no eye liner or army boots."

That was a low blow. "Skeletons can wear boots and eye-liner."

"You're not a skeleton, Cain; you're death personified."

"And I'm deadly in boots, eyeliner, and a duster."

"We've told you already; you're free to save up and buy your own duster."

"Why do you guys hate my duster idea so much?"

"We don't hate it, Cain; we're just robe people, that's all. And when mean girl at school call you a Satan-worshiping warlock, will you please not agree with her, and then take a joke way too far until she cries?"

"I didn't make Ivy Skelton cry. I doubt she has human emotions. That other little overachiever girl cried, Aurora something-or-other. Besides, if you and Father really know Satan, as you claim, you'd thank me for standing up for your friend, but okay."

"If you hate the real world with humans so much, then do the work and get a plan together to reap your next soul. Study. Practice. Reap. Then, you will control your fate, and you will be able to choose to leave humanity behind and traipse about in the ether for as many centuries as you want. But your father and I haven't seen you do the required work yet, and we have yet to see you give humanity a real try."

"I've been trying since I was five."

"Cain, we raised you as a human to give you perspective on life before an eternity of doling out death. It was never a punishment."

"Well, humanity is disgusting and it feels like punishment. And I look forward to removing them one by one for all of time."

"That's big talk for a kid afraid of the eternal flame."

"You know what?" He closed his book. "Fine." Cain landed both his socked feet flat on the table so hard that the original iron hardware of the old door clanked. He climbed over his homework.

Mom followed him into the basement, through the secret

door, lower and lower through catacombs into the Library of Forbidden Knowledge to watch her son find a soul to take.

Cain dreaded discovering who he was bound by fate to kill. But he was worried more that he wouldn't be able to complete the assignment without his parents' help.

MaKayla

Sometimes, a present, if it's cute enough, can plow through the darkest rain clouds with the brightest of colors and change a person's whole outlook. Especially with wrapping paper, a super-well-done bow, and a precious accent like a heart sticker or an origami. So hopefully, the fifty minutes MaKayla had already spent on wrapping a dollar store poppable fidget-spinner hadn't been wasted. Besides, MaKayla needed the distraction from the other package as much as she needed to make peace with Ivy.

And sure, Ivy Skelton had been an absolute jerk to MaKayla since the third grade, but maybe the two young women were just one immaculately wrapped tchotchke away from becoming best friends. Well, maybe not *best* friends; MaKayla's best friend was . But hopefully Ivy and MaKayla could become close.

MaKayla thought of the perfect, most precious accent: a unicorn eraser that was exactly like the one she used back in third grade. Besides, what if jealousy of that very eraser was what originally put a wedge between them all those years ago?

Maybe MaKayla was getting a tad hyper-focused on mending her conflict with Ivy as a means to ignore the inevitable knock-down-drag-out fight with her mother, but she could forgive herself for that. At least she had an actionable plan to improve ties with Ivy, whereas she had no idea what to say or do about her mom except stare at scissors and cry.

So, with a couple of glue dots, the unicorn eraser stood atop the short, square jewelry box on the light green wrapping, between the brown ribbon ends, looking away from the tall heap of green bows. MaKayla knew Ivy was really into trees, so the wrapping was made to look like a giant old tree with roots snaking away. And all the wrapping was made of recycled paper *and* was compostable. Ivy was going to love it. She just had to.

Would she love it enough to forgive MaKayla for rear ending her in the school parking lot, making Ivy late for visiting hours to see her dying grandfather? That remained to be seen. Who could truly know the future? Certainly not MaKayla Colfax. All she could do was her absolute best gift-wrapping on a token of friendship and hope nobody told the principal.

With the fidget spinner wrapped and all her homework done, MaKayla felt the familiar pull of social media to scroll through, cute outfits to see, friends to be jealous of, bottomless holes of informative or hilarious videos to fall into. But there, on her bedroom desk, sitting right next to her phone were those damn scissors that couldn't cut paper, fabric, string, or even hair. Practically worthless, except MaKayla figured they might be actual silver.

She'd tossed them in her desk for the time being, planning on running them to the local flea market to find out what they were worth. Hopefully. Who didn't have dreams of being told by some expert that an old piece of junk was actually a priceless historical artifact? A girl could dream...

MaKayla was certain she put the shears in her desk drawer. But here they were, on her desk again.

Was Aaron breaking into her room? She'd already had to

upgrade her bedroom door locks once he passed double digits in age. Something in their chemical makeup turned little brothers into grabby-handed gremlins when they hit a certain age. She didn't even resent his snooping—she just made sure to be mindful of it. And if he was going through her desk, was he looking to steal her anxiety meds? No, he knew she kept them in the bathroom. So was he looking for a diary? MaKayla didn't keep one specifically to avoid snooping.

So what could her little brother have been looking for in her drawer?

Wait.

When did MaKayla pick up the shears? And when had she polished them?

She looked down at her shirt. Her pretty pink blouse was now streaked with black smudging stripes. Somehow, she'd absentmindedly polished the scissors clean with vinegar. But when had she gotten her bottle of vinegar out of her crafting closet? MaKayla tried to remember, then caught herself rubbing the scissors blades over a handful of her pink blouse again.

Suddenly, a sharp headache blared behind her eyes, scrunching her forehead and blurring her vision. Lines appeared, like streaking light stretching out from the sun. Or like taut golden wire catching the light from her over-bright desk lamp.

Wasn't this what astigmatism was supposed to look like? Was she too young for that? Did MaKayla need some kind of surgery?

No, it was stress. Had to be. Stress or more side effects from anxiety medication. She pulled out her bedroom desk drawer and placed the shears among the ocean of markers and pens, waves flowing each time she opened the drawer. She pushed the drawer closed, imagining her shears and pens crashing back into an invisible sea inside her desk.

But that was just like MaKayla, always imagining something that wasn't there, dreaming of the grand hidden in the mundane. Old scissors from a crazy relative was an unbelievable inheritance. Her desk drawer held an ocean within, and tiny gifts she spent too much time and effort on would be appreciated and loved and would pay off with true real, deep friendships. One day.

Who was she kidding?

Maybe MaKayla was separated from reality. Maybe it ran in her family. She'd ask her mom after talking about scheduling an eye appointment.

MaKayla grabbed her phone and headed downstairs to join her mom and dad on the couch watching terrible TV. Before she turned off the too-bright lamp, she glanced at the shears on the desk.

But...didn't she just put them away?

Ivy

"What in the hell's a warlock anyways?" Janet—Ivy's birth mother—was at the end of her rope. And dear gods, hopefully at the end of her current tirade.

Ivy went back and forth between stifling laughs and yawns as 'Mom' (that's what Janet called herself) regurgitated quotes from what Ivy assumed was the last parenting book she read.

Of course Janet wouldn't know what a warlock was. She didn't even understand who her own father was. And if it were him sitting here, Grandpa would know what type of warlock, where from, and the capabilities that idiot had.

If this Cain kid even was one.

And honestly, his little monologue at school about magic and turning Ivy into a toad was pretty funny, as well as startlingly accurate. Plus, you didn't get the name Cain Morrigan without at least one parent with a penchant for the occult.

So, as per usual, Ivy kept her mouth shut and listened.

She sat on the uncomfortable kitchen chair, not eating the delivered dinner, nodding in empathetic agreement with her mother's great communicating. Under the kitchen table, she rubbed the newest rune to have appeared on her leg. It burned, but it was a good burn, just as Grandpa said it'd be. The kind of pain makes you a better person on the other side.

With five runes, it wouldn't be long now. As soon as Janet shut up, Ivy could move onto the next incantation to begin the next rune. She and Grandpa's plan was finally coming together.

Ivy smiled.

Janet said she was happy they were on the same page with open channels of communication.

Ivy stifled another laugh.

The rune burned. She couldn't wait to show Grandpa.

Chapter 3

Cain

Despite what any religious text claimed, fire was the first communication directly from a deity to man. It was like an apology gift. *Sorry for the lack of fur, hide, tusk, fangs, horns, antlers, or claws. Here, have a chemical reaction.* And for mankind, it was the perfect advantage to have over all the animals who naturally had some or all of those gifts.

The cool, blue light of the eternal flame made the Library of Forbidden Knowledge even spookier. Unnatural shadows danced around the stone shelves filled with scrolls, tomes, and skulls.

Cain's mom was a very dramatic decorator. She dressed much simpler in her robe and the faux fur-lined moccasins specifically kept for the walk down.

If she were heading down alone to consult the flame, she may have used her non-corporeal form, making her decent quickly. The fact that she didn't signalled to Cain that something was bothering her. He just didn't know if it was the call from school or something to do with the next soul he was to cull.

To begin, Cain relaxed into his true Reaper self. Existing as a human actually took a good amount of concentration. Forcing your body into an odd, unnatural form was an active task; converting back into a corporeal form was like falling back into a soft, fluffy bed.

His features hardened, calcifying into the happy sneer of a human skeleton. Unlike his mother's, Cain's Reaper form had not yet become permanent, settling into something new with each shift. A more stable Reaper form was something he would earn eventually, along with his own eternal flame. And maybe a cool prop like a scythe or an hourglass.

Until then, he was a new set of bones, elongated and un-adorned, standing before a blue flame on a pedestal, reciting a spell written before words existed.

This was his favorite part. He *was* a goth kid, after all.

The flame grew and grew until it engulfed Cain's boney Reaper form. Before him, the eternal flame revealed the identity of the next soul he would take from its earthly vessel.

It wasn't a name or an image, or even a family tree to look at. It was the person's identity, which included the self as well as all connections, earthly and otherwise. Souls were tied to worldly possessions as well as a web of living people. Usually, the soul also would have a couple strings pulling taut from above, like flying several kites. Those were ties to dead friends and relatives, or even God for the religious.

But this guy, this soul whose identity slowly revealed itself to Cain, had very few ties to earth, maybe a couple heartstrings for those kept close. Instead, he had dozens and dozens of lines reaching up, away from the land of the living. And these ties weren't the normal taut golden lines that Cain had seen. No, these were jagged wires, loops, forks of upside-down lightning, and festoons of limp rope.

"What is this?" Cain said aloud as he walked around the vision within the expanded blue flame.

"What dost thou see, mine son?" Mom, too, had shed her humanity, standing as a giant skeleton, her black muslin robe tattered and flapping in the breeze from the eternal flame.

"His ties... He has so many. And almost none of them are earthly."

"Ah, the pious pilgrim. Maybe a student of the divine. He would be quick to join his creator, methinks."

"But these aren't ties to his heart. They aren't the normal lines."

"Speak of them to me."

"There are many and varied. Some are twine of other colors, some heavy drooping rope. And even fingers of electricity reaching for the sky."

"Egads," Mom whispered to herself. "Withdraw the knowledge thou seekest and let us discuss."

By the time Cain had memorized every aspect of the soul's identity and spoke the incantation to return the eternal flame, Mom was back to her dark-haired, hazel-eyed self and sprawling heavy ancient texts spread across the library's tables.

All the tables in the Morrigan household were repurposed doors from fallen castles, forts, churches, and other strongholds. After all, Reapers rejoiced in the folly of man reaching for the infinite, especially through architecture. Sieges and buildings falling made for busy Reapers, so Cain's parents took doors. The giant log door tables surrounding the eternal flame were now overlaid with a collection of ancient books.

By the time Cain returned to his teen guy form and cracked

open a sports drink, Mom had each book open to pages that depicted the very ties he'd seen in his visions through crude pictures.

In the books, he read that the lightning shooting from the soul to the great beyond linked to long-dead gods. One book explained that multi-colored strings to the beyond were debts owed to the dead that transcended earthly existence. Such attachments, the book explained, were often deals with the dead in exchange for knowledge. Other books went into greater detail about which color meant what type of bond. It turned out this particular soul had made many a deal with the already passed.

But in none of the open books, or even in the scrolls Mom unfurled, were the heavy, drooping ropes mentioned. They remained a mystery, as if the soul were an anchor to many mysterious ships too tall to behold.

"He is going to be difficult," Cain said, frustrated that the answers he needed weren't in the old texts.

"Then we won't tell Father about it." She winked at her son, but when he didn't return a smile, she understood the seriousness. "Is it because the soul is infirmed?"

Cain shook his head, fixated on an ancient drawing in the cracked brown paper page in front of him. An image of his father, the ink-black Reaper touching a dying man, looked up from the shadow of its hood, out of the book, at Cain. "This soul is old. On a respirator. He's been bed-bound for months. But no, there is something about his ties... They're unnaturally strong."

"Well, yes, he has blood debts beyond this world."

"Not just those ties. His earthly ones. Or maybe just the one. To his granddaughter. It shimmered with power. She is the anchor that keeps his soul on Earth."

"This will prove difficult. Definitely do not tell your father about this."

"And there is one more thing. You know that girl at school who said I was a warlock, and then I got in trouble for threatening student's pets? Ivy Skelton?"

"Yes?"

"She's the granddaughter."

MaKayla

She'd never been in a fight in her life, but Ivy Skelton seemed hellbent on throwing down. MaKayla literally didn't know what to do as the short brown-haired girl began removing earrings and bracelets.

"They said I was too late. Missed visiting hours." Ivy Skelton was scary as hell, speaking slowly and calmly while staring daggers of fury into MaKayla.

"I am so sorry, and—"

"I had dinner with my mom. I *hate* my mom. Now we have brunch this weekend." She said it like brunch was a vicious threat.

A crowd had grown in the underclass parking lot, kids hanging around longer by their cars to watch the confrontation.

Well, now was as good of a time as any.

"...and I got you a little something. To say sorry." MaKayla clumsily retrieved the small box from her backpack, her ears burning in embarrassment under so many eyes. Her hand shook as she held the immaculately wrapped gift out at arm's length toward Ivy. MaKayla hadn't had enough anxiety medication this morning to get her through a parking lot fist fight.

"'Sorry' won't give me time with Grandpa."

"Please." MaKayla managed a forced smile. Nobody had ever rejected one of her tokens of friendship before. Her Mom had taught her that a thoughtful gift given in public could resolve any dispute. Or was that just another of Mom's lies? MaKayla's voice went up way higher than she meant to when she added, "I worked really hard on it."

The anticipation from onlookers had grown. Most kids had their phones out and were recording, hoping to catch a beat down on video. MaKayla really didn't want her first fight to go viral.

But then Ivy relaxed out of her fighting stance and tilted her head curiously. She approached the little gift, studying it. MaKayla relaxed. Ivy's move from ready to throw down into interest really turned off the crowd, who groaned audibly. Most kids put their phones away and headed to homeroom.

"How long did you work on it?" Ivy snatched the wrapped package away from MaKayla and studied it.

"The wrapping? Maybe almost an hour all together."

Ivy made a disappointed face then pushed at the little unicorn on top. "And what's this?"

"That was the eraser I had on a rainbow pencil back in the third grade when we first met."

Ivy's eyes studied MaKayla's incredulously. "You've had this since the third grade?"

MaKayla smiled harder and shrugged. "Yeah?"

Ivy plucked the unicorn off the package and tossed the rest of the gift on the ground. "Watch where you're driving." With a serious hair flip, Ivy marched away toward the main building.

It wasn't the most appreciative reaction to a signature

wrapped gift MaKayla had ever experienced, but it was loads better than getting punched in the face. So Mom might have been right about this one.

MaKayla took a breath to recover and double-checked to make sure no one was watching anymore. With her first step toward homeroom, she heard a metallic clatter at her feet. The shears.

She quickly fell to a knee and shoved them back into her bag.

She'd never put them in her bag in the first place, though. There was no way she grabbed them out of her desk. And there was no hole in her bag for the scissors to fall through.

Or was she just this forgetful? These shears were stressing her out, a reminder of her mother's dishonesty, that she was going to have to confront Mom at some point. But that had to come later. She'd just narrowly avoided her first fight, she couldn't add any more pressure right then.

The bell rang, so MaKayla had no time to figure it out. She forgave herself again for forgetting about putting the shears in her bag. Maybe there was a mental block around the antique scissors. Maybe she had unprocessed feelings about her estranged grandmother that Ivy's Grandpa was stirring up. Maybe every problem she'd ever had with her mother seemed perfectly summed up in the fact MaKayla thought her maternal grandmother had been dead since MaKayla was five. Whatever the reason, MaKayla had been forgiving herself a lot over the mysterious shears.

Self-forgiveness had recently become a pretty important part of checking in with herself. In middle school, MaKayla's pursuit of perfection led her to the school nurse with multiple panic attacks. After a couple therapists, each with their own coping mechanisms, the coping tools that MaKayla chose to keep were the anxiety cup and deliberate self-forgiveness.

Walking into homeroom with a deep breath, clenching and relaxing her shoulders, MaKayla forgave herself once more.

At least Ivy accepted the gift...kind of.

MaKayla figured that would be the end of any unscheduled excitement of the day.

It would be a busy day; she had to compare notes for history and chemistry all during homeroom, then quizzes in chemistry and history, she had to finish her introduction during lunch for her Advanced Art collage getting graded today, plus she'd promised to help her book club friends with their posters, which she planned to do during the last two periods of the day. Those were classes she already had A's in anyway.

She snaked through the busy halls, smiling and catching greetings on her way to the lockers. Seville High School was laid out well – one wide, oversized H in two stories. And all of her classes were on one side of the letter, where most upperclassmen were.

But MaKayla's locker was with the other sophomores, across the bridge of the H. She could have asked to move lockers, but it was really the only way she could still see all her friends. So she took the long way across the school to trade trig notes for history, returning an edited art history essay in exchange for chemistry notes.

But the headache was back and just killing her. Too much stress. Did she need to take another pill? But then, she noticed she was about to walk into something and almost fell over to avoid it. A chest-high yellow bar floated down the hallway, moving diagonally toward her. It passed above everyone else in the hall, but none of them noticed.

When it was less than foot away, she saw it was more like

a thin line, a wire maybe, glowing a bit. She ducked before it could clothesline her.

The wire passed over her head smoothly, but still, no one else noticed it. Of course, everyone did notice her ducking and covering her head.

Under the burning hot attention, she straightened up, pulling at her professional-looking blouse, realigning the straps on her book bag, and adjusting the grip on her silver shears.

Before she had the opportunity to question again the replacement of the heirloom, she saw another line, this one dimmer, going up straight to the ceiling.

Trying to look conspicuous while both checking out the glowing line and confirming that still no one else was seeing it, MaKayla forced a smile and hurried toward the endpoint of the wire.

She scooted around a couple crowds of kids to see Mark Cecilia, her friend Ora's boyfriend, grabbing books and closing his locker. Normal high school kid things...except for a faint, glowing line pointed upward from his head to the ceiling tiles.

There was nothing else weird about Mark; nothing else glowed around him. Just a regular high school jock headed down an emptying hallway, unaware of the wire now coming out of his shoulder. Sure, his smile was part cringe, but that's because MaKayla was gawking.

Oh, crap. MaKayla just got caught gawking.

And for some ungodly reason, to play it off, MaKayla turned and literally whistled as she sauntered off. Wow, what a completely natural thing to do. She even held the shears behind her back under her bag as she meandered off.

Real smooth.

But the glowing lines didn't stop. Colors from orange yellow to a shiny gold, snaking about at odd, changing angles like thin carousel poles, all moving above their hidden anchors. And as the halls emptied out, more and more of the threads became apparent, now moving between the walls and ceiling.

MaKayla reached out to touch one, and she felt it in her hand—a taut string. Without explanation, her mind went to the school's softball team, how close they were and how patient the coach was. MaKayla pushed the intrusive thoughts aside and focused on the thread, feeling how tightly the fibers were drawn. She walked along the hall, feeling the string pass through her fingers, watching all the tiny spun fibers radiating golden light impossibly, thinking of how attractive the softball coach was.

But wait...MaKayla never found the high school coach attractive before. She was so thrown, she let go of the thread, and immediately forgot about the coach. Then she noticed she'd walked into another thread. No, not into, but through. The thread poked out on either side of her like she'd walked through laser pointers aimed at each other. She shifted her attention from the chest high thread going down the hallway to the one running across it at hip height and—

The second bell rang, jarring her. She had to get to home room and now, but she couldn't help it; she had to reach out for the second string.

She felt it within her grasp. But how? A moment ago, she'd passed right through it, like some hologram.

She gave it a tug, but it was stuck. And her thoughts rushed to that freshman couple who was always making out in the cafeteria.

What was happening?

She put down the shears carefully, right next to her foot, taking a mental picture of them sitting on the linoleum floor.

Then she reached up for the string…but it was gone.

All of the strings were gone.

Huh.

Was it possible she imagined it?

Well, she was stressed over the busy day ahead of her, she thought as she began her inner monologue, preparing to forgive herself. But she had to get to homeroom.

So she grabbed the shears and took a step toward homeroom and…

All of the strings were back. The yellow wires ran diagonally from wall to door, the goldens spanning the length of the bridge hallway. All completely taut. All glowing.

MaKayla looked more closely this time. She got in there. And they were made of thick thread. Like twine. Honest-to-God glowing twine running all crazy conspiracy investigation board throughout her high school.

A shoe squeaked behind her, and only then did MaKayla realize how she must have looked, crouch-walking through the hallways, looking at something nobody else could see. Her whole body heated up in embarrassment, and she didn't turn to see who had caught her as she pushed through the stairway door up to the homeroom.

Cain

Cain was the worst student in school as a matter of pride. He was deliberately late to class, behind on homework, and absent from all events. Sure, maybe part of it was laziness or simply not seeing the point in good transcripts for a guiding spirit of the dead, but he considered it a social experiment. Would a community tolerate a misfit? Would a school properly perform its function and nurture a young mind despite resistance or incompatibility with modern education? Would teachers empathize? Would students accept him?

So far, all the answers had been a resounding no.

It wasn't that Cain had absolutely no friends or was some social pariah. He hung out with the smokers while skipping assemblies (even though cigarettes did nothing for him), he laid around the small campus with the stoners (even though Reapers, even in human form, didn't really get stoned), and he even lunched with the less-popular wing of the book club.

But at the end of the day, nobody got too close. No one got a full picture of who Cain was. And that was by design.

So it wasn't unusual that after being late to homeroom and witnessing a sophomore girl having what would appear to be a full-on mental collapse, he bolted from Seville High and went back home to skip the full day. Only Cain knew it wasn't a mental collapse he'd just witnessed.

Nobody understood as well as the Reaper-in-training that appearances were often misleading. The girl, McKenna, Cain thought she was named, wasn't imagining things or having a stress-induced episode. She was seeing human connections.

Lovelines, or heartstrings as Mom called them, were among the many things Cain saw that most mortals couldn't. Cain could perceive his parents in their Reaper form, which humans generally couldn't. But he could also see all sorts of other paranormal things: ghosts roaming the Earth, auras, even curses or spells. There were lots of things normal humans were oblivious to.

So how could lovelines be perceived by a totally normal sophomore girl McKenna? Or was it Kendra? Kaylee? Camilla?

Her name didn't matter. She was just another hot girl who went to his school and cared way too much about high school drama. What mattered was that this bubbly girl with a wavy mane of dark hair and piercing eyes who definitely smiled too much could glimpse the world that was supposed to be Cain's alone.

And the impossibility of that frustrated Cain to no end.

He spread out a whole new set of ancient tomes and scrolls on door-tables in his parents' Library of Forbidden Knowledge. Both parents would be out culling souls all day, each powerful enough to keep an eternal flame with them as they flew from dying person to dying person.

Cain skipped enough school to understand how to not get caught.

But sifting through old books, trying to find facts about love-lines and how mortals perceive them, was a nearly impossible task. Maybe paying more attention in English class could have helped the young Reaper's research. Maybe he should have paid attention to lectures about the importance of primary sources, how to follow the scavenger hunt that was footnotes, or how to search indexes.

Nah. This was just a mystery that Cain had to power through.

Of course he asked the magical spirits of the library to help, but the results were meager. A book in Aramaic discussed the ties that prophets and supposed messiahs had with their disciples, and how many of those disciples claimed to have had visions of the ties to their leaders. A scroll from ancient Egypt revealed that Cleopatra claimed to perceive love between her subjects. An ancient guidebook to Hinduism claimed that by in believing the interconnectedness of humanity, a human could eventually learn to view those connections.

But there was no way this random girl from his school had achieved the level of spiritual clarity required to see such things.

Cain kept reading, kept flipping ancient pages with gloved fingers, kept getting more and more frustrated while looking back and forth between books.

He found nothing else that could explain how a human girl could see earthly ties. But he did find an answer to a question he hadn't asked himself about a more pressing issue, something specifical he didn't want to think about: the soul he was charged with taking.

That soul, covered with ties and strings and anchor points, held its brightest, strongest, and more power-imbued connection with his granddaughter. A bright, golden, shimmering connection. A connection that Cain now recognized as an enchanted loveline.

But wasn't that impossible? The target soul didn't just have some connection; it was *anchored* to the physical world by a loveline, a connection somehow imbued with magical power.

Lovelines shouldn't be that special, that powerful. Humans could remain connected to one another through life and death; it wasn't as if people stopped caring about each other once they passed. But how could a loveline be an anchor point keeping someone alive? He had to learn more about the assignment's Earthly ties, but the answers weren't in these books, they were in a hospital bed with the old man.

He slammed a fist on the door-table.

He got a thrill out of the clanking sound of the ancient hardware, but he was really getting frustrated.

Cain took a breath and tried to think of what Father would do. Certainly, the most powerful Spirit of Death in North America wouldn't get completely thrown by a human who could perceive earthly ties.

Of course Father wouldn't; he was the perfect Reaper, the end-all-be-all, strong enough to manage the flow of the river Styx. He even had the Beginner Reaper's Guide memorized from reading it to Cain, even though it'd only been published a couple years back.

That was when Cain realized what his father would tell him if he were there: go back to the basics.

He passed the various translations of Necronomicons, huge three-by-five foot books, readable by only the most powerful, he pulled a small trade paperback off the shelf.

"So, you're a Reaper?" the title said, alongside a cartoonish Death shrugging, sickle in hand. Again, the book wasn't old, but it was extremely well-read, enough cracks running up the spine. Mother had added enough tabs poking out to make the thing look fringed.

Cain turned to the chapter titled "So what happens to *them?*" The book was modern and conversational (this annoyed Cain, who preferred a bit of elevated language, especially when dealing with such elevated concepts) and read as follows:

And what about the poor souls collected? Do they wind up spending eternity wearing wings and strumming harps upon clouds? Or maybe roasting with all of the more interesting people in fiery caverns? While the actual answer is a lot more nuanced than these simplistic concepts (and vary particular to each soul passing), there are a number of things we do know:

Those who survive keep memories alive, not only maintaining but even at times strengthening bonds of love over time. Bonds of family, admiration, mutual respect, romance, or even lust will stay in place forever no matter where souls go. In truth, the only ones capable of destroying such bonds are the Fates, the often-studied but seldom-proven humans charged with sustaining the complex weave of human relationships.

The existence of Fates is often debated. We know from ancient texts that they once existed, even after the conquering and assimilation of ancient Macedonian and Greek cultures. But the fact is, there hasn't been a documented account of a human who can perceive and control bonds such as lovelines, lifelines, or scourges in over a millennium. It is safe to assume that Fates no longer exist.

Fates could destroy such bonds.

A thrill rushed through Cain. Not only had he found another powerful, supernatural being, he'd also proven his father's favorite book incorrect. That sophomore girl, whatever her name was, was a Fate.

And a Fate was just what Cain needed to cull his target soul.

Chapter 4

MaKayla

She couldn't bring herself to turn off the car, and she wasn't even finishing a bop to jam out to. No, today had been so "capital W" W-E-I-R-D, she was still processing it, and definitely didn't want to talk about it with Mom.

MaKayla was a cruddy actor and a worse liar, so depending on how much her mom asked about her day, MaKayla would most likely wind up telling on herself. So, she sat in the car, engine, air conditioning, and music off. One hand tightly gripped her steering wheel like she was hanging by a rope for her life.

Her other hand carried the shears.

No matter how often she put them away, they were bound to show back up, falling to the ground, appearing on a nearby desk or countertop. Worse, was when they suddenly showed up in her hand, leading MaKayla to wonder if her grandmother's antique shears had some impossibly supernatural powers, or if MaKayla was beginning to lose her grip on reality. And the headaches didn't help.

MaKayla really hated second-guessing herself like this. She took pride in her prioritization of her mental health in the two years after the anxiety attacks got bad. Her first step had been no longer using the term "crazy" when she meant "wild." And that also went for moods; she wouldn't even let herself think that she was going crazy. That term wasn't helpful. Crazy wasn't a concept to use lightly and was never helpful. But dear God, what was going on in her mind?

The question chilled her insides and mixed them up at the same time. It was like standing at the edge of a cliff, looking out onto a misty body of water and knowing the danger of being so close, but drawn to the mystery of whatever was out there in the fog. Whatever it was, it was calling to her.

Or her medication was no longer helpful, and MaKayla shouldn't be trusting herself.

What she shouldn't be doing either, was hanging out in the car for over half an hour when her mom could see her from inside their home.

So, she made a decision. Walking into the house clutching a pair of scissors like a weapon was a bad idea, so she put on her light Seville High School jacket and stuffed them in the pocket. Hopefully, that was close enough to her to prevent the inanimate object from acting up. Just in case, she pressed a hand against her pocket as she entered her home.

"Hi, hon!" her mother called from the other room, bringing some fresh flowers in a vase to the front room. They were from the garden, of course. She had a green thumb that she'd talk about to anyone who'd listen. "Is it that cold out?"

"Yeah, I guess. I've got to go work on my art project..."

"You didn't get a bunch of paint all over a really nice top I bought again, did you?"

That was Mom, worried more about appearances than how her daughter actually was. But now Mom's superficiality was insignificant in comparison with everything else on MaKayla's mind.

"No, Mom."

MaKayla dropped her backpack and carefully removed her jacket.

Mom gave her the side-eye. "Alright, alright. How did your quizzes go today?"

"Good..."

"Well, that 'good' didn't sound good."

"I don't know. We'll see." She held her scissors through her jacket pocket while carrying her book bag.

"Is there something going on that I should know about?"

"No, it's just..." Then MaKayla saw her opening and went for it. "Yes, actually. I was wondering if I could go back to seeing my therapist."

"Therapist? Is everything alright?"

"My medication just might be giving me headaches, that's all." MaKayla used the line as an exit, rushing upstairs.

"Are you sure there? Is there anything you want to talk about?"

"Yes. To my therapist." MaKayla knew she was walking a thin line between a firm boundary and one command too far for Mom.

They stood for a moment in a stare down, MaKayla at the top of the stairs and Mom down in the foyer.

"Well, okay, honey. I'll find her number." Mom had a way of speaking about the most important things in a flippant tone, something that usually infuriated MaKayla. But this meant Mom was willing to end the conversation, even if it was with a huge guilt trip, "If you wanna do it, let's go ahead and do it. I want you to feel nice and healthy and everything, but I especially want you to talk to her before you have another bad day when you have two quizzes."

"Thanks, Mom." MaKayla desperately tried to walk to her room, but Mom's voice caught her again.

"Dad and Aaron will be home after baseball, so dinner won't be until seven."

"Okay, Mom."

"I love you. Go work on your homework. I've got to clean up the kitchen after massacring these lilies."

Makayla had managed to talk to her mom and get out of there without giving away that her entire world was a big trippy question mark right now. Plus, MaKayla's need to talk to a therapist was about a million times more dire than she made it sound.

Just as MaKayla closed the door to the refuge of her room, letting out a deep sigh of relief, she felt the itch, the immediate urge to make sure the shears were okay. She needed them in her hand for reasons she didn't understand.

But holding onto them now came with a wave of guilt. Yes, Mom had been dishonest about her grandmother, but did that make being dishonest back the right thing to do?

MaKayla needed that therapist fast. That felt even more true while staring at all the work she still had to do on her art collage—the fine points of her self-portrait were currently just scraps of paper and ribbon. The problem was that MaKayla didn't want to put down the one pair of scissors she owned that weren't going to help her finish her collage.

Then came *The Screech*. The Screech was well-known in the Colfax house. Aaron and MaKayla called it that because, one, it sounded like a screeching animal and, two, because whatever direction everyone's day was going, it suddenly hit the brakes and swerved.

"MaKayla (secret middle name) Colfax, you get back down here this instant!"

When Mom was really mad, she called out like this, then waited silently with arms crossed at the bottom of the stairs or even in the living room to make MaKayla sweat about why she was in trouble as she rushed down.

But the moment her mother saw her, words overflowed from Mom's mouth, shaky quivery words like the water at the edges of her eyes. "When did you get this?"

In her hand was the brown wrapping covered in inked stamps that had contained the shears.

"I don't know, like two days ago."

"*You know!* Don't lie to me!" Mom's words were half-screech.

MaKayla was immediately so uncertain and small, she felt nine years old. "I just got a package; it isn't a big deal."

"Stop lying!" Mom slammed her fist onto the pedestal table at the center of the foyer. It wobbled, sending the fresh-cut lilies toppling over and the crystal vase rolling off the glass, shattering into wet chaos on the marble floor.

MaKayla stood stunned. That was a six-thousand-dollar vase—Mom had made sure she and her brother knew that. That vase, purchased after one of her big business deals, was a top tier possession, a decoration serving as a point of pride for the whole family.

And Mom didn't even notice it broke.

"It was scissors, okay?" MaKayla's voice trembled as she gripped them tight behind her back. "Just a stupid pair of scissors. They don't even work. They can't even cut anything."

"Is this why you want to see your therapist?"

"No."

"Don't you lie." Mom's voice fell to never-before-heard depths.

"Okay, yes."

"Get down here *right now*," Mom whispered as she turned abruptly and marched into the living room.

MaKayla followed, her mom plowing ahead past the seating area, marched down the hall, and walked into her and Dad's bedroom. Without turning, Mom pointed to a chair and headed off into her walk-in closet. "Sit down."

MaKayla obeyed, placing the shears underneath her thigh as she sat. The contact with them was almost comforting, but the second her fingers let go of the handles, her hands flexed, and her palm tickled, yearning to hold them once more. As her mother made noise rustling through her own closet, MaKayla forced her hands onto her knees. Her belly filled with a building anxiety that could only be expressed through a shifting antsyness.

Cain

While training to be an immortal force of nature, Cain learned to recognize his own limitations. Up until now, he'd approached each culling with hesitation, letting his humanity get the best of him. But now, with a Fate's help, he could easily harvest this soul, complete his assignment, and live the rest of eternity as a Reaper.

Except, of course, he knew nothing about Fates. And judging

by how the books in the Library of Forbidden Knowledge discussed Fates, nobody really did.

This assignment was going to take a little extra effort on Cain's part. While he loathed the concept of homework as it pertained to school, he could assign himself some extra work to guarantee a successful soul harvest.

So before he would even approach the Fate girl, he had to learn as much as he could about his assignment. He knew Ivy Skelton, a classmate of his since he started attending Seville High School. She was weird and a little gothy like him, even though she could tolerate the other students, staying involved in clubs and organizations. But he knew nothing about her family.

Then the plan began to formulate. First he would learn as much as he could observing the assigned soul, then he would approach the Fate. Judging by the way she reacted to the lovelines at school, he doubted she understood her powers. He could use that...offer to help her gain control and understanding of her powers. Cutting the lovelines of his assignment would just be Fate practice.

This was actually a pretty good plan. Maybe Mom was right; he hadn't been applying himself enough to become a reaper. But now was different. Now he was doing the work. He slipped out of the house to spy on old man Skelton.

MaKayla

Mom had obviously never wanted to talk about her mother, the grandmother MaKayla never knew. But to get angry with MaKayla for lying when Mom had lied first was elite level hypocrisy.

MaKayla wasn't going to call Mom a hypocrite—that wasn't their relationship. Dad could do that; he'd get away with it.

"This is my own fault." Mom's voice was a husk of a tired whisper. She stood at the threshold of the bedroom, still in a gray yoga suit, but now she wore kitchen gloves. She held onto an old cigar box like she was carrying a case of jewels. "I did my best not to scare you or burden you, and that meant not always being forthright with the truth."

You think?

"But now I can no longer shield you from the truth. The women in our family, Corinthia women, are cursed. Doomed to go insane. When I was twelve, my gia-gia took her own life. It was...messy. Lots of blood. I remember for years after, visiting Papa, I'd find old dark brown spots along the floorboards in corners. She killed herself with these."

Mom delicately placed the cigar box on the bed. It was covered in carvings, burnt scrawls of letters in other languages, patterns of doodles that no sane person could have the patience to lay down. With a quiet creak, Mom opened the box, revealing a dazzling pair of gold and copper shears. They were completely different from MaKayla's. Mom's scissors were fat and ovoid where MaKayla's were long and lean. The pair in the box more resembled gardening shears and looked as much when Mom looped gloved fingers into the handles and picked them up. She made a few practice snips at the air.

"After Gia-gia's funeral, they showed up in my room. Someone left them there for me to find. They had..." Tears almost overtook Mom. "The person who left them for me had my name inscribed into them. Into the blades that killed my Gia-gia."

"Did you find out who it was?" MaKayla asked, understanding that she couldn't entirely believe her mother's answer.

"I did. I did because madness bubbles up. It can't stay hidden. And I'm sorry I tried, MaKayla. I'm sorry I tried to hide it from you."

"Who gave you the scissors?"

"Oh, honey. You know who."

"My grandmother?"

Mom nodded. "My own mother told me that... She said that scissors made her closer to God, and as long as she didn't let go of hers...she was going to live forever. And she told me that if I held onto mine and never ever let them go, I could stay with her forever. And I...I tried to talk to her. To tell her it was crazy, to just listen to herself—she was talking crazy! But she just left them with me. And when I tried throwing them away, she'd hide them in my room again. And she denied it and said that it was God bringing them back to me and that I'd never understand or be happy unless I just...held onto them."

Going to therapy, dealing with her own issues, MaKayla had grown careful of using the word 'crazy.' And hearing her mother tossing it around, she would usually have said something. But Mom was right. MaKayla shifted to sit on her hands, touching her fingertips to the handle of her own...of her grandmother's shears. The metal was warm. The smoothness, the *feel* of them was a small relief, scratching the edge of an itch when the skin aches, burning for more.

Mom was crying now, pushing through the words and streams of tears, not breaking. As if she wouldn't surrender control enough to sob. MaKayla had never seen her mom so emotional, but it was so like her.

"This went on for days. All she'd talk about was the scissors and my destiny, our fate. She stopped eating, threatening to leave the family whenever I wasn't holding them. And the scary part was, she was kind of right. It felt good to hold them; it calmed me. In the midst of Gia-gia dying and then my family about to fall apart, the only time I had any peace was holding those damned scissors. She'd convinced me that I needed them until they were the only things that could comfort me. Eventually, there was only one thing to do. I called child services on her. She and Dad, your grandpa, never officially got a divorce, but I lived with him until I graduated. She wrote to me for years. But it was always about the scissors. She'd ask about mine, then complain about how they took hers away.

"Then one day, the letters stopped. I assumed she died. I didn't mean to lie. I just...I meant to withhold information, hoping that I'd finally beaten the sickness that took my grandmother's and mother's life. But it's back, isn't it?"

MaKayla could only nod. Not only was her guard completely down, hearing her mother open up like never before, but now there was the underlying threat that if MaKayla lied any further, her mother might call someone to take her away like her gia-gia.

"Were they etched with your name?"

MaKayla nodded again.

Mom's face contorted, squinting to hold back tears but afraid to ask, "Do they...do they call to you?"

This time, MaKayla cracked. The quivering dam of her grimace broke, sobs escaping her mouth, tears pouring from her eyes. Again, she nodded.

"MaKayla, I know I kept this from you, but please understand I thought I was protecting you. Because I can help you. I can show you how I stopped the calling of the shears. But you have to trust me."

She thought long and hard but realized she had no choice. There was no one else who would believe her except Mom. If she told anyone else, Dad included, she'd wind up just like her grandmother. But even with Mom knowing, understanding, having experienced what MaKayla was experiencing, it was different for Mom. And the difference left MaKayla so alone.

Without a choice, she said, "Okay, Mom."

Through bleary eyes and a cracked, broken voice, Mom was suddenly excited, pitching an idea in a business meeting. "This may sound crazy, but I believe that this box has the power to quiet the scissors. It's not magic or any kind of science, but I believe it, and it works. And it can work for you, but only if you trust me, and only if you believe it works."

Still gloved, Mom placed her copper and gold shears back in the box. Then she cleared her throat and said gently, "You have the scissors with you, don't you, MaKayla?"

"Yes."

"Put them in the box, honey."

At the offer, MaKayla didn't hesitate, reaching for her shears while getting up. She understood why her mother lied, understood in a way no one else could. They had both felt the pull of the shears, the unnerving, unraveling feeling of not being able to trust themselves, to trust their own minds. Only they had felt themselves slip through their own fingertips, their thoughts belonging to something else. Part of them was now what a pair of shears had put in.

And Mom had a way out, a way to make the shears stop beckoning her.

But the moment they were again in her grasp, her fingers wrapped around the wide silver grip, MaKayla felt a thrill. Holding the shears felt *right*. And Mom was trying to take that away from her. Suddenly, it was such a stupid idea—throwing this powerful gift away, severing herself from this wild and new side of herself she'd never known, cutting herself off from her only connection to her grandmother.

MaKayla never even had a nickname for her own grandmother. She didn't know if she should think of her as Nana, Grandma, Grandmom, Gam Gam? It would be hilarious if it weren't infuriatingly tragic. MaKayla wondered what she was really like and if her grandmother knew anything about her. Suddenly, the room brightened.

There was already one string in the room—a strong, thick, straw color going into and through her mother's gray sports top, thinning out to the width of a thread, its color indiscernible as it ran down beneath MaKayla's chin. But another string, thinner yet brighter, appeared, lighting the room in a warm yellow. From the same anchor within MaKayla, the bright new string pointed up through the ceiling. And without reaching for it, MaKayla already knew it connected her to her grandmother.

If she wanted it, MaKayla was suddenly certain that she could cut the line with either pair of the enchanted shears in the room.

Or she could put hers away, lock them in a box, and cut that line without ever even using the shears.

"Whatever you're thinking, it's not you. It's thoughts from the shears. And nobody but me is going to believe that. This box is the only help I have to offer you, MaKayla. Please."

MaKayla's heart split into warring factions, siding with and against her mother and grandmother each.

She didn't remember walking over to Mom, but she remembered sobbing as she dropped the scissors into the cigar-box. They fell from her hand like a fifty pound weight, so heavy that MaKayla detected an unfairness when they landed with a light tinkling sound against her mother's shears.

The lid snapped shut. Her mother turned and swept the box away.

MaKayla felt emptied from the chest out. The pull of absence was close to cracking her rib cage open. Instinctively, she stepped back, leaned away so she wouldn't be sucked into the closet after Mom. MaKayla pulled back so hard, she fell to the thick carpet floor, weeping, her shoulders spasming with body-shaking sobs.

Her mother never came out of the darkened closet.

MaKayla cried and cried until she didn't. Even though there was no door separating them, MaKayla said nothing to her mom. That wasn't their relationship.

She picked herself up and walked back to her room.

Ivy

She read Grandpa his favorite Crowley journal, then sat quietly in a chair as he drifted off. There was another hour to visit, so she scrolled through her phone, doing homework. The real stuff, not the high school indoctrinations. She was reading the US Constitution, but not for patriotism (which is stupid; if you're going to align with an enormous cultural team, why not pick something cooler than Christians and Muslims and Agnostics? Ivy would rather pit the human against the monstrous. The living vs. the dead).

No, Ivy had learned from Grandpa how to scan historical documents for clues left behind by secret societies of the occult. Words that stood out, that didn't conform to the writing norms of the time, could be strung together into a code, a message to the future.

These were some of the most powerful spells, Grandpa had explained. The old man had a library full of historic texts, renowned works of literature and eccentric collections of specific nonfiction. The secrets of the occult were scattered throughout those books, but they were still socially acceptable to own. Nan wouldn't think twice about inviting anyone into her home who might casually glance at her book collection.

The tomes that had been bound in human skin, cursed and powerful, she kept hidden in the floorboards. All the knowledge Ivy was heir to, a miniscule portion of the inheritance of the supernatural she was due. Whenever Grandpa passed away for good.

But they both knew that wasn't going to happen for a long, long time.

"Hello, you son of a bitch." Grandpa spoke to the empty, shadowed corner of the room.

Ivy's skin crawled. The confidence of Grandpa's voice...the power he managed to put behind it, the authority... It wasn't the ramblings of a dying old man. He saw something in the dark. Something supernatural. He was talking to someone Ivy couldn't see.

Cain

Cain shouldn't have come. He knew he shouldn't have come, even just to learn more about his target, but he lied to his parents and came anyway. Now he was stuck, frozen in the corner of the hospital room. It was impossible for the elderly man to have seen him, and yet...

He had no idea what to do. Hide? Vanish? He was an oddly shaped Reaper form at the moment; he could have simply stared Grandpa Skelton down with an other-worldly glare.

Only Grandpa Skelton wasn't the scared one.

"You are an angel of Death. I identify you, Reaper."

Painful fear overtook Cain's chest. The old man saw him. How?

Cain Morrigan withdrew into himself, falling into his own mind just as his mother had taught him. He'd been transitioning between planes of existence for as long as he could remember. Before baby Cain was confident toddling about on his own feet, he knew how to fall through his own mind into the Realm of Beyond.

For once, the cold, isolated, completely lifeless Realm of Beyond was comforting to Cain. He'd escaped. He could catch his breath. Gather his thoughts.

What had he done wrong? Nothing. It was a culling like any of the other dozens of souls he'd taken. He should have been able to reach into the old man's mouth, forehead, or chest and remove the spark of life.

But he hadn't gotten anywhere near the bedridden old man before Cain got spotted. It was impossible. Cain had done nothing different; he had transitioned between realms to bring his Reaper form toward his target. It had all gone exactly as it had for every other culling.

The only difference was the target. The soul. The wildly golden thread from the soul to his granddaughter. The shining golden bond, unlike anything he'd ever seen before. That's what was so different about this soul. That's what made this target unlike the rest.

Cain couldn't put words to how he knew it was true, but he

knew it. Something about the light coming off of whatever that bond was revealed his Reaper form to the old soul.

But suddenly, there in the endless Realm of Beyond, Cain was not alone. Nobody else was there, but instead, a presence. Something, someone had followed him.

"Are you 'feared of me, demon?" Grandpa Skelton's wet, dragging voice came from everywhere and nowhere all at once.

Floating among the deep purples of cloud and shadow and fear, Cain spun about to find how someone else had gotten into the Realm. Then he saw the mouth, disembodied in the ether.

Faded, yellowed teeth like antique light bulbs against unhealthy pale cracked lips demanded, "What are you? Some lesser Reaper, a child? Or is Death so clumsy? Have I come to the end of my journey only to find my fated adversary inept? A mindless tool of wanton gods? What are you, a servant or neophyte?"

Here in the Realm of Beyond, Cain had no physical body, only a sense of who he was, a combination of his skeletal Reaper self and fleshy human form. So, it made no sense when he went cold with fear, his throat too thick to swallow, his skin chilled and prickly.

"Has Death underestimated me, or am I only worth the work of a lickspittle?" Grandpa Skelton dragged words along his muddy gravel voice.

Something gripped Cain's neck. Despite lacking a body, Cain felt pressure around his throat, tightening. Then he was flung, ripped from the Realm of Beyond, through his own mind, and into his human form. The hospital floor rushed up to hit his face. The force sent his forehead slamming to the floor, causing a very tangible pain that woke him up to the danger he was in.

No. It couldn't be. Nothing like this was possible. A human, reaching into the Realm of Beyond and dragging out a Reaper? It was so ridiculous, it would be funny, if it weren't so terrifying. This human, this mortal soul, was more powerful than a Reaper of Death.

Something was still wrapped around his neck, although not so taut. He reached and pulled it away, tugging the glowing rope up over his head and clear of his own body.

Grandpa Skelton was on his feet now. Frail, with paper mâché flesh, strewn with cords and tubes. But one cord, unlike the others, glowing, crackling with power, came from his chest and had looped about Cain's neck.

The old man pulled Cain up easily and stared him in the eyes.

Cain panicked and fell away again, out of the stranglehold of the shimmering golden loveline.

"Death cannot touch me, Lickspittle. Not so long as I have this."

The greasy, rocky words echoed as Cain descended through his mind, this time running, hiding, falling through realms and dimensions and planes of existence. Running through all manners of reality and not daring to look back at whatever that human was.

He didn't stop until he was back home in his room.

Not so long as I have this.

Chapter 5

MaKayla

MaKayla wandered into the next day without her usual shield and armor of preparation, overdone homework, and the thought and care it took just to be an extra student. Not today. She was out of her element, reacting. Like the whole school day had taken her by surprise and all she could do was try and keep up.

Yesterday wasn't just a mental and emotional odyssey but also a complete wash as a student. Her life was out of control, as was her mental health for the first time in years. The only person who understood, her mother, had withdrawn into her own issues.

The only thing MaKayla could control at that point was her studies. So walking into school, she had her mind set on catching up. She traded more notes, zoned out instead of finishing essays, and wrote an art proposal. She absolutely bombed her project introduction yesterday. She was itching for her scissors the whole time, so she pretty much begged for any chance to do extra credit.

When lunch came around, MaKayla spent her time sketching a companion piece to her art project. Her preferred medium was collage, so her sketches weren't the best to begin with. But today, her mind couldn't keep still.

No matter her attempts to focus, all thoughts eventually led back to the scissors. It wasn't just thinking about them or even the itch to touch them, MaKayla coveted the scissors. It was like lust — just the thought of the sensation of their weight in her hands got her a bit light-headed; made her hungry to hold them.

And for a moment, a thought crept up from her periphery like frost on a windshield. What if Mom's cursed box wasn't strong enough to hold her shears? What if the box was only strong enough for one pair? Or what if it didn't work at all?

This sketch was a mess. So were the earlier crumpled up attempts.

Her original project had been so simple. A quest narrative, the little girl moving from home through a fantasy world just to come back changed. The companion piece was supposed to be an older, wiser woman looking at her own reflection but seeing her young, naïve, former self.

But nothing she drew worked, and her spiral-bound sketch pad was getting thinner and thinner.

"Narcissus," a smooth, self-assured, masculine voice pointed out from beyond the table.

MaKayla didn't look up. She pretended she didn't hear, starting a new page. When she found an empty table in the corner of the cafeteria, her friends had gotten the hint, but she should have anticipated that some bro douche wouldn't catch on.

"You know, everyone thinks he was such a beautiful dude,

but in reality, he was ugly."

"You know," MaKayla replied without looking up, "the school banned earbuds to cut down on cheating, but in reality, it's led to *way* more white guys butting in when they're not wanted."

"All I was saying was that I like your art."

"Thank you for telling me. Now I know not to believe in your opinions on art. My sketching is God awful."

"I'm sorry. I'll leave you alone. It's just that when I see art that affects me, I feel it like someone pulling on one of my heartstrings." He over-pronounced the last word.

MaKayla wasn't listening, though, still not looking up."When does the leaving me alone part start?"

"Just paying you a compliment. Have a good day."

What an absolutely infuriating answer.

"Just creeping on sophomore lunch break to pick up younger girls? Have the day you deserve, buddy."

"My name is Cain."

What the hell was wrong with this guy? MaKayla didn't have the mental bandwidth for this today and shot him down hard. "Cain Morrigan, I know. The junior most likely to become a school shooter."

That jab landed. Cain's composed swagger stiffened as he mumbled, "Wow. Okay..."

Crap. MaKayla wanted to hand out a clear rejection, not bully a kid who was already a social outcast. Besides, she didn't really think that and didn't need that kind of comment defining her. "I'm sorry; that went too far. It was needlessly mean, and I apologize. I should know better. But I still want you to leave me alone and think I have made that clear for a while now."

Thankfully, he left without another word. But of course, that made her feel even worse.

MaKayla sat in her own rotten thoughts, stewing silently except the scritch-scratch of her pencil on her pad. She was shadowing the reflection, the older and wiser character of the piece.

There was no way Cain Morrigan knew anything about what she'd been seeing, the fight with Mom, or her mental connection with the old scissors.

Her itchy palm tickled, then hurt, then burned, yearning at the thought. The tighter she gripped the pencil, scratching on the thick paper, the more she imagined snipping a string.

A taut twine, invisible to everyone but her, running straight into that emo poseur Cain's chest. She pictured herself grabbing hold with her left hand, opening the mouth of the shears with the singing grate of metal on metal, and pressing the apex of the shears' wide mouth against the twine.

Snip.

The sensation, the satisfaction, the slide of blades closed... It was all a promise from the inanimate scissors.

What had he said? A heartstring? That's what the twine connections were like, and she had to cut one. She just *had* to.

And specifically, she wanted to snip the heartstrings that connected Mark and Ora.

The pencil scraped graphite against the paper.

She envisioned the shears in her hand, the graying twine connecting the hearts of Ora and Mark, her fingers wrapping around the taut line and...

Snip.

The pencil tip broke, and she snapped the rest of it in her hand. How was she out of breath? Was she sweating? And why did she suddenly care so much about her friend Ora and Ora's boyfriend Mark?

The sketch was trashed. The mirror the young lady looked into reflected back a completely darkened room. The reflection of the blackness, the void of a room, broke the very edges of the mirror, escaping into the young lady's reality. Darkness tearing into her life.

The more she looked at it, the more MaKayla liked the sketch. Not only had the heroine changed on her quest, but her home was no longer recognizable.

The bell rang, snapping her out of her reverie.

She cleaned up the chaos of her rejected drafts, stuffing them into a recycling bin and everything else in her backpack. As she put her phone in her pocket to leave, the slightest inkling of the snip of her shears resonated within her hand.

Did Cain Freaking Morrigan really trigger her that bad?

Cain

Okay, so the first attempt at recruiting MaKayla went poorly. Which didn't make a lick of sense, because Cain had spent years studying the behavior of adolescent boys, and his approach was completely socially acceptable, if not exemplary.

He had even washed off his eyeliner and nail polish. And for what? To be treated as some ignorant bro? Cain seethed. He could read over twenty languages and spoke six, four fluently.

She did apologize, at least. But did everyone at school really think he'd become some murderous shooter? The thought sat sourly with him, even though ironically, he'd most likely be the one to take all of their souls one day. Still, he'd never kill someone as a human. That was insulting.

"It's Connect Four, Cain. This isn't 3D chess," Mom said. "That's later."

Cain snapped out of it.

The other end of the long door-table was filled with games at which Mom had already defeated Cain—Chess, checkers, peg checkers, Settlers of Kataan, Cards Against Humans. He was used to losing, against either of his parents. It just usually took a long time. Today, he and Mom had flown through games.

He slid a red circle down the yellow vertical game board, but his attention was nowhere near the game. Mom's black game piece slid into place. She'd won.

"Connect Four. Okay, fine, you're released from family game night. We'll call this one a wash. Next night your father is home, though, we'll make sure to have a game night." Mom began boxing up the pieces. "How's the assignment going?"

Cain played it nonchalantly. "I'm taking my time. Stopping and doing research before jumping in."

"Good! That's smart, Cain. I couldn't help but notice that you were reading up on heartstrings. Are you nervous about the connection you saw in the Eternal Flame?"

"No, just curious."

"Okay, fine." She gathered and stacked all the game boxes. "But just so you know, Shiva and Devi can cut Earthly connections. And I think there are ancient Egyptian enchantments that can imbue scissors with those abilities."

Carefully, Cain asked, "What about a Fate?"

"Well, yeah, if you can find one. But I'm not aware of enough people practicing Ancient Greek Polytheism to empower a young woman with the capabilities of a Fate. Cain, I know you're reticent to ask for help, but..."

"Because if I ask for help, you'll make me stay human for

another decade."

"Don't be so dramatic. You'd be human for another five years at most."

"I don't understand how you can stand it, being in this embarrassing, fleshy body so much of the time."

"One day, I hope you do understand it. Humans are amazing creatures, not in spite of their short lives but because of them. You and I may have near eternity to do the things we want, create and nurture the relationships we seek, but a human must constantly prioritize, whether consciously or not, just to fit a life into their small spans. Because when their time is up, their time has to be up."

That last line was a dig at Cain, and he knew it. He still had days to harvest Grandpa Skelton's soul, but it was finite time. Every second that ticked away was another second Cain lost to cull.

So, he did the unthinkable. The absolute last thing Cain thought he would ever be caught doing.

He texted one of his classmates.

MaKayla

MaKayla was amazing at faking a good mood for the sake of customer service. It was one of her superpowers. Anyone who came into Lockport Arts and Crafts not only left with what they needed, but they also had a sense that simply by asking the high school girl stocking shelves, they'd somehow made her day.

Nobody was making MaKayla's day today.

Even though it wasn't the same, she kept a pair of teacher

scissors in one hand while she worked. No matter how hard she squeezed the closed mouth of the comparable shears, it didn't scratch the itch.

She even went to the wrapping section and snipped samples of twine, ribbon, and string. But it wasn't the same. It wasn't what her hands *really* wanted.

MaKayla was really beginning to wonder if her mom's little magic box was working after all.

"Where can I find paint?" an elderly woman asked. She had disgust on her face, looking MaKayla up and down.

"What kind of paint? We have lots of different ones: acrylic, oil, water, gouache..." MaKayla loved that word.

"Just show me the regular paint!"

"I'm not sure which—"

"Now! Unless you want me passed out in your messy aisle here."

Fine. MaKayla stopped stocking birdhouse kits, leaving the only box in the "messy aisle."

On her way to the side of the store with most of the paints, MaKayla asked what the woman was using the paints for and found out she was looking to rust-proof an old outdoor metal chair. "This is an oil-based acrylic, perfect for metal."

"But I don't want it to rust."

"This will help with that."

"But it doesn't have rust in the name." The woman pulled up her glasses and read the label from an inch away. "Where does it say rust-proof?"

MaKayla didn't have the time or eyesight to read the fine print on the back of the can. So she picked up a cheaper, inferior paint with big black letters that read 'Rust-Proof.' She smiled and pitched her voice high and cheery, "This looks like what you're looking for!"

"I don't know why it took so long," the old woman muttered, as she shuffled away without so much as a thank you.

And then immediately, Ora, MaKayla's best friend and co-worker was all over her, complaining about boy problems.

"If you knew that Mark was cheating on me, you'd tell me, right?"

"Of course, I would."

"Okay. Well...is he?"

MaKayla was too tired for this. She answered with as much interest as she could muster. "Ora, I haven't heard anything."

"Okay, well, I'm pretty sure he's cheating on me."

MaKayla envisioned a frayed gray string coming from Ora's exposed deep ocher chest and how satisfying it would be to snip.

"Ora, that absolutely sucks," MaKayla said, and walked back to her project. It was back to stocking birdhouses.

But Ora and her worries followed.

"He keeps liking this other girl's pictures on her profile, and last weekend, he went to St. Paul Academy's baseball game without me. And I think he's back to smoking pot again"

"And that makes you think he's cheating on you?"

To be honest, Ora's drama was a welcome change of pace from the nightmare MaKayla was currently living. As much as Ora cared about her relationship, nobody was going insane or covering up a death. Ora's drama was much more easily digestible than MaKayla's.

"That and he's like super-secretive with his phone, and he never used to be."

MaKayla did her best to listen actively, nodding and mh-hming with all of Ora's points, all while stocking the birdhouse kits. But then the whine. The high-pitched nasal sound like Ora's teakettle of emotion was boiling.

She was crying, full-out sobbing, by the time MaKayla could stand and reach out for a hug.

"Are you sure you didn't know?" Ora asked through tears. "He said you were staring him down in the hallway. I thought maybe you knew something. He said that he thinks you don't like him because he's a jock, but I'm afraid he's just planting a wedge between us in case he has to deny it if you told me he was cheating. So... are you sure he's not cheating?"

"Ora...I don't know."

"Okay."

"If you're so sure he's cheating, why don't you dump him?"

"Because we're destined to be together."

Ora had always said that about her and Mark, even before they began dating. For a while, MaKayla took it as a manifestation of a goal, and frankly, she was proud of her friend. She wanted this boyfriend—Ora had set her sights and spoke it into reality. But now, this talk of destiny was some pipe dream that was keeping Ora in a toxic relationship.

"So, what are you going to do?"

"I'm going to sleep with Jeremy Lonnergan."

"Oh, Ora. Don't."

"No. I've already decided. Jeremy likes Black girls, and Mark hates Jeremy, but they all hang out with the same paint-balling guys, so Mark will def find out."

"You *want* him to find out?"

"Eventually. Like way after I do it so it can be something I apologize for, and he'll apologize for cheating on me, and then we can forgive each other and start over."

"And that sounds like a healthy relationship decision to

you?"

The question was left unanswered, and MaKayla returned to shelving birdhouses.

"So, why were you staring at him in the hallway?"

Thinking back, MaKayla didn't feel guilty or even nervous about lying about seeing Mark's attachment, the string protruding from him and most likely running up to Ora. It was the only lie that was easy, since at the heart of it, MaKayla didn't think it was real.

She wasn't lying when she denied the strings existed because most likely, they didn't. Most likely, MaKayla had inherited mental instability. So, not telling her best friend about the scissors, the thread, and the fight with her mom didn't feel like dishonesty.

All MaKayla felt was the urge, the need, to sever that cord. She longed for the singing snip of shears on twine, the sound echoing around her brain. Separating Mark from Ora.

"MaKayla?"

"What?"

"Why *were* you staring at Mark?"

"I don't know. I thought I saw something on his shirt, but I was wrong."

It wasn't *technically* a lie.

"You're certain you didn't know about Mark cheating or hear anything about it?"

"Ora, I'm terrible at lying, and you know it. Nobody tells me secrets."

That was absolutely true.

Her phone vibrated once more. A double buzz this time.

Usually the best employee about not checking her phone on the sales floor, MaKayla ripped her phone out of her pocket.

Anything to get out of this uncomfortable conversation. She opened the message from a number she didn't recognize and froze.

Who sent this to her?

How did they know?

Right there in plain letters read the message: "MaKayla, I know you're seeing things. I can help."

Her stomach solidified into a frozen mass of fear.

"MaKayla? Hello? Did you get bad news? Everything okay?"

"Yeah...I'm fine."

"You *are* bad at lying. You look like you just saw a ghost."

"I've just got a lot going on right now."

Like going completely insane because a pair of scissors were planting thoughts in her head, and the only people who knew about it were her mother, who lived permanently in denial, and this mystery person texting her like a blackmailer from a horror movie.

"Sorry. I didn't mean to dump on you when you were down." Ora was genuinely a good friend. MaKayla felt bad for not sharing with her and only made it worse because she wasn't helping Ora with her relationship problems.

"It's okay. Just don't do anything rash about Mark until you're certain. Or maybe talk to him...or like, break up with him if you want."

"Thanks, MaKayla. You're a really good friend, but you just don't understand destiny."

MaKayla had the sinking feeling she was about to find out a lot more about destiny than she ever wanted.

Cain

Despite what his parents, the smokers at school, and most of his middle school teachers would say, Cain was confident he knew when to apologize. And if he was going to get the help of this girl, if she really was a Fate, he'd have to apologize to her. He had to be his true self, completely honest. If Death was going to continue to be a balancing force in the universe, Cain had to reveal that that's what he was.

"Can I have a word with MaKayla?" he asked the other girl working next to the young Fate. The other art store employee may have gone to their school, too, but he wasn't sure.

"Um, what do you want?" The girl's voice dripped with judgment. Disgust at him, yeah, but she was also talking about her coworker as if she wasn't there, akin to some possessive boyfriend.

But MaKayla seemed to appreciate it, stocking shelves from a case on the floor but nodding behind her friend.

MaKayla didn't even look up. "I don't have anything to say to you, Cain."

Her coworker stood, unmoving. They were a united front, staring him down.

Cain hated this about humans: the willingness, or compulsion even, to align themselves with others. Families at least made sense; most animals kept family or even community units. But humans *wanted* specific allies for everything.

He really didn't want to explain himself to more than one human, but if he had to eat crow to complete this assignment, if that saved Death from Grandpa Skelton, then Cain would be vulnerable. He would be earnest. He cleared his throat. Twice.

"I, um... I should... I guess I need... I have to apologize to MaKayla."

She still didn't look up. "Not interested, bro."

"She says she's not interested, bro."

"I, uh…I misrepresented myself earlier. Because I… I stupidly thought you liked guys who talked like that or treated girls… women like that. Well, I don't treat women like that. I lied, I acted differently, and I shouldn't have. This"—he gestured to his face, now looking more like himself, complete with eyeliner— "this is me, and I'd like to talk to MaKayla for a second. Please."

The speech at least worked on Ora who finally broke their united wall of rejecting face and turned to MaKayla to see if it worked on her too. Whether it did or not, MaKayla sighed, rolled her eyes, and groaned to the point that she looked in pain. She then nodded without enthusiasm or sincerity but rather exhausted resignation. But that was enough for Cain. It was a chance. And he had to get a Fate on his side.

MaKayla

This was literally the last thing MaKayla needed. Her plate was full — her mind pulled her in tons of directions. Her therapist would have said that her anxiety cup was spilling over.

And now there was this puppy dog of a boy following her around.

Admittedly, his confession and apology would usually have worked wonders on her. Nothing like true vulnerability to make a boy look like boyfriend material. Not just an apology, but an explanation as to why he'd been a jerk, really looked good on a guy.

And this guy didn't look half bad on his own.

It couldn't have just been the little outline of eyeliner that improved his appearance so much. He was right—this was the real him now. Putting on whatever character he was trying in the school cafeteria made him look...doughy, down to a fake smile unnaturally pushing his chin and cheeks, or even his eyebrows trying so hard to create a smolder, they could have cramped from overuse.

But now, his big orphan eyes drew her in. His combination of pale skin and the almost-frail thinness of a high school boy, new to his tall body, accented high cheekbones, and long neck which made him look even taller. But this gauntness gave sick Victorian boy vibes, and MaKayla had to resist the urge to get him some soup and a warm blanket.

Still... his height and his shoulders struck a heroic silhouette. And those lips. No white boy had any business with lips like those, a roller coaster of curvature from a loopy Cupid's bow to the steep drop-off of the deep dip of his lower lip.

Crap, MaKayla was staring. And she'd already waved Ora off for privacy, so there was no downplaying it. She didn't need any more stress from boys fishing but definitely didn't have time to swoon back.

"Like I said, I'm not interested, bro."

"Ah, well. I'm an only child you see. And most people would find me very un-bro-ey."

"What do you want?"

"Truthfully?"

He peeked around the corner, checking either side of the aisle, crossing his hands in front of himself as if it made him more inconspicuous.

Who was MaKayla to judge? She literally whistled and skipped away sometimes. It was kind of nice to have this meaningless conversation humoring this emo himbo instead of the crushing weight of everything else that was so serious demanding her attention and mental well-being.

His eyes went from searching the aisles to daring her as he whispered the accusation sharply, "I know."

He gestured scissors with his fingers.

Scissors.

What was this? How big of a secret was she just now being let in on?

She immediately played it cool, letting out a silent breath and casually side-eying him. Had she gasped when she saw his gesture? She couldn't tell. Had she given away that she knew what he was talking about? That it scared her to see him mention this dark secret of hers in public?

"What do you know?" She tried to act confused or uncaring, but her voice cracked.

"Yeah, good try." He was very dismissive, which suddenly rankled her in surprising ways. His tone switched to professorial. "We need to carve out some time and find someplace safe where we can experiment."

"Experiment?"

He stumbled over the words to correct himself. "Test out, or...try stuff. We need privacy but within a populated area. We need to see your capabilities."

"What capabilities?" she tried to say as naturally as possible.

"Has anyone told you you're bad at playing dumb?"

"Why should I trust you?"

"Because now you know that I know your secrets, which are ancient and great. Knowledge forbidden to humans."

"That's not good enough."

"You can trust me. I'm here to help you through this."

Here to help? It sounded a little too much like Mom, but

only a minute ago, MaKayla thought her mom was the only other person alive who knew. Suddenly, the secret didn't feel so personal, so specific to her family. If others knew...maybe there was a lot more than just scissors and strings to learn about.

"Wait, are you here to...to train me?"

He hesitated, then answered confidently. "Yes."

"But you've been going to Seville since freshman year. Was all that a cover?"

"Yes."

"Well, why didn't you just say that?"

"It's not how I would phrase it."

"I can't believe you tried hitting on me as your first approach."

"That was regrettable."

"You should have befriended me like...at least last year."

"Perhaps, but what's done is done, and I'm afraid we are on a schedule."

"What kind of schedule?"

"Can we meet? After you get done here?"

"No, I have to go straight home after work."

"Then can I meet you in your room?"

She must have made a face because he quickly corrected himself.

"To talk, just for a few moments. Just to make a plan."

"You can't sneak in. I'm on the second floor—no trees."

"I can get in."

"My dad will flip out if he catches you."

"He won't. MaKayla, believe me, he can't." The sincerity in his voice was unmistakable. This was a deeper truth he was admitting, much like admitting he wasn't the bro that had hit on her earlier. She believed him; all of it, everything he'd said. She believed him absolutely.

He was someone different than she'd ever imagined, something different. He was full of forbidden knowledge beyond the sheltered existence MaKayla had in upstate New York.

Now, his very presence thrilled her. Some box of some kind of feels deep in her chest opened up, and she didn't recognize the sensation. Like standing close to a horse for the first time, amazed at the majesty of an animal and afraid of the deadly threat it posed by simply existing nearby.

That awe dried out her voice, more wind than whisper when she asked, "What are you?"

The question must've bothered him, wrinkled his face. He spoke like he had a bad taste in his mouth. "I don't know how much I'll be able to tell you."

"Then I won't know how much I'll be able to trust."

"That is fair. Tonight." He half-bowed and backed away.

"Wait." Her own voice surprised her, but one question was burning her mind and wouldn't wait until that night. Again, she asked something that terrified her, afraid of the answer but filled with the sheer scale of the possibilities that lay ahead:

"What am I?"

One corner of his mouth pulled in an amused grin. It was like he shrugged but with his face.

"Fate," he said simply and walked out.

And MaKayla didn't know if she'd ever forgive him...

Chapter 6

Cain

If Cain was going to spend the rest of eternity traveling through realities, unbinding souls from their earthly bodies, he couldn't be this nervous every time he had to go into a girl's room.

Recruitment of the young Fate had really turned around; after blundering through the conversation at school, they seemed to really hit it off in the art store. Not that liking her was necessary to the plan—whether they got along or not was immaterial. Social compatibility was a positive that had the potential of making the culling of Grandpa Skelton easier, though. It was a positive, just like the fact that she happened to be pretty, or that she seemed as if she were the only student he'd encountered at Seville High who listened, actually listened to him when he spoke and didn't just wait for him to stop talking so she could blurt out something, or even worse, scroll through her phone while pretending to engage.

Cain brushed the idea away. Interest in the Fate beyond the assignment was superfluous. Even considering his feelings for her as positives was dangerous; attachments were nothing more than liabilities, strings that could be pulled to make a puppet dance.

Cain was no human's puppet.

He felt very human right now, however. His stomach was queasy, and sweat beaded on his forehead as he looked out into the dark night. He couldn't imagine being cooped up like a normal human, stuck in one little town, with only one angle of the vast sea of stars to watch. He was always grateful he could see the sky around the world, through the magic-sensitive Reaper eyes, or even from different planes of existence.

But tonight, the night sky just reminded him how dangerous he was making this mission.

How could he even be considering telling this girl who he was, *what* he was? It was sacred knowledge; a deeper truth than any human encounters in the span of an average lifespan.

But this was no average human. Or was she? From the sounds of things, she'd only discovered this other side of her recently. She was *new* to this. All of her thinking was still rooted in the material, the facade of the human world—and worse, the world of American humans.

He would be fine. As always, around these humans, Cain would keep his guard up. She was a neophyte at the occult; he was the expert. But if that were true, then why did he have to repeat it to himself over and over to keep his heart rate down? Flowing through the night sky in a darkened Reaper form, merely the whisper of a shadow drifting as darkened fog, the very human sensation of anxiety rattled his thoughts.

Not that he needed it, but the second story window on the north end of the house was open with the light on inside. Of course it was; MaKayla was one of those humans constantly searching for and trying to understand the feelings of others. Even when Cain was acting like an absolute jerk to her, she still apologized when her words crossed a line.

As if words could hurt Cain...as if he were some vulnerable human teenager.

But it was easier to flow his darkness through the window rather than fall through realms and back into this one within her bedroom walls. And he'd never admit it, but he appreciated MaKayla's gesture to leave an entry open and a light on.

MaKayla's room was not what he expected. The white walls were covered with clippings, so much so that one entire wall was one big collage. Cut up pictures and cloth, all in a range of black and white, like a grayscale kidnapper's note overtaking a room. But each image interacted and played, one clump of portraits here connected by drawn wind gusts and fabric-cut cloth clouds to a frankesteined city of photos and textures. All of it, the whole room, was one big piece of art. One narrative, pasted piece by piece across her living space. Something Cain suddenly needed time to digest, to analyze, to translate for himself.

Being here, seeing these walls that had taken so much work and such vision, such confidence in one's specific perspective... It was altogether intimate, much more personal than witnessing someone's nudity. Cain felt as if he were seeing some truer portion of MaKayla, something she wore her human body over.

Cain found himself staring, taking it all in while still in his shadowed form. Not noticing him, MaKayla sat on the floor on a bohemian patchwork rug, big headphones to accompany homework with way too many books. She was one of those who supplemented school texts with library books. The pile toppled outward from either side and was strewn across her pink-on-black bed.

As intrusive as being in this room felt, Cain had no problem staring at her through his enhanced vision. As a Reaper, even in shadow form, he could see so much more—earthly ties, auras, the history of each part of her, the energy of an exploded star still pulsing within each atom. But it was the very human, very delicate, and small details about MaKayla which intrigued Cain.

Her head bobbed, stray curls springing from symmetrical buns. As she read voraciously, near-black eyes whipping back and forth down each page, her jaw periodically flexed. An innocuous enough spasm, but it sent a tightening down her neck, showing the stretched ligature surrounding her throat lit in stark relief on her sand-tone skin and, for an instant, the well of concavity resting above her clavicle dipped deep.

He was staring. He didn't notice until she noticed him. And when she noticed him, she freaked out.

Her eyes jumped out toward the shadow that was Cain. He wasn't a normal shadow. He was *the* darkness, the true darkness that humans feared within the mere lack of light. True darkness was unknown and unknowable, filled with unspeakable dangers, and above all, unstoppable.

MaKayla's face gaped and warped in a grotesque muted shriek. Tears overfilled her eyes. Her skin blanched in terror.

And Cain realized that not only was he staring at her, but she was frozen in abject terror of him.

He stepped out of his own shadow, into MaKayla's bedroom, onto her bohemian rug. The effect on MaKayla wore off in an instant. Her face relaxed to normal, if not accusatory, with knitted eyebrows casting uncertainty in Cain's direction. "Can we not do that again? You were...nightmarish. I don't want to see anything like that ever again."

"Oh, child, there are terrors, much more frightening terrors, out there you have yet to encounter."

"Why do you talk like that?" She still sat against the side of her bed, white headphones now around her neck, judgment on her face. "And don't call me 'child.' What are you, eighteen?"

Cain had always thought his speech, coupled with his otherworldly presence, gave him an agelessness. Or at least he'd pass for much older.

"I'm seventeen," he admitted.

"*I'm* seventeen," she pointed out.

"Okay, apologies. But there's still a lot I can teach you. Let's start with lovelines."

"I can't see them."

"You can't? Why not?"

"I don't have my shears."

"Well, we can't start anything without the shears. Where are they?"

MaKayla

It was the first time she'd ever called them *her* shears. They were hers, and she talked about them like something she owned like a great key chain or some other thing that wasn't a big deal, not the physical manifestation of a generational curse (or mental instability). But Cain didn't blink. He must have known what the shears were, what they were doing to her, to her mind, and he volunteered to help get them back. In fact, he was hyper-focused on it.

Whatever kind of shadow monster Cain Morrigan was, he

knew more about what was happening to MaKayla than she did, maybe even more than her mom knew.

So she answered all his questions.

Yes, Mom was most likely asleep.

Yes, Dad was in the living room.

No, Dad didn't have any guns in the house.

The walk-in closet was the open doorway off the main bedroom on the first floor.

Yes, she was sure there were no guns in the house.

But after MaKayla had answered all of his, she found he was much less accommodating to her own questions.

How could he find the enchanted box if it were hidden?

How could he get downstairs, through the bedroom, and into the closet without disturbing Mom or Dad?

Was he sure he could open the enchanted box, even if he found it?

He evaded her interrogation entirely with apologies for what he couldn't explain. But this was the guy who was supposed to have answers for all her questions. And even if he was being the silent mentor-type, he didn't have to be such a jerk about it.

Maybe her questions frustrated him. He must have been expecting some brown-nosing perfect pupil. And while, yes, MaKayla was in fact in the top 5% of her class, she got there by questioning and learning on her terms. Any subjects requiring blind obedience were always her weakest.

So, this mentorship to master her powers and take control of this birthright of hers was bush league. But honestly, this toxic expectation of a doting and obedient disciple was pretty on-brand for the guy who said he faked being a douche bag because he thought she'd be attracted to him.

This dude was practically made of red flags. But MaKayla wasn't interested in him. Or at least, she could box up and put away any parts of her who might have wanted that. MaKayla needed his know-how. What had he called it? Forbidden knowledge.

She longed for it. She knew that the truth about her was in the darkness most people couldn't see. But he wasn't going to reveal that knowledge if she didn't comply.

Perhaps that was why she couldn't look away when he asked her to, when he morphed, turning into the darkness. The outline of him, his shape, the slight distinction of light determining where Cain ended and the rest of the room began, grew. His shadow overtook him, swallowed him up, poured about him from impossible angles, drowned him in depths. And then all that was left were depths, a shapeless nothing, a shadow in the middle of her room, staring at her with shiny-nickel eyes.

But it wasn't the form of a man. Cain the guy was gone, and in his place, a void absorbed the light where Cain had stood. And the sight of it somehow spoke directly into MaKayla's mind. When she looked into Cain's darkness, the invading thoughts were deeper, more aggressive, more obtrusive than even the shears. Seeds of doubt sprouted, grew, put down roots and built canopies all in high-speed time. Fear, painfully born into some horrible form within her mind, doubled and redoubled.

Immediately, MaKayla realized she'd most likely be failing all of her classes throughout the rest of her high school career. Socially, everyone would come to understand that she was nothing but the worst parts of her mother, stitched together poorly in an ugly package. Further, MaKayla came to realize that she was not as strong or smart as her mother, that her own madness would control her in a way her mother had learned to tame. That her mother, with all of the faults MaKayla had identified, was a best-case scenario in dealing with their destinies, Mom was a mark MaKayla would never live up to. It was a height to which she aspired but would continually fall—unable to reach the lip of the cliff side, she would topple down, fall into mediocrity, and plummet into the darkness of disappointment.

Then Cain's shadow form disappeared, and MaKayla immediately felt much better. Though she did have a newfound anger at herself for her curiosity. Anger at knowing that no matter how many times she was burned attempting to gain forbidden knowledge, she'd continue to seek it out.

Out of habit, MaKayla forgave herself. She refused to tolerate self-loathing. And deep down, she understood that no matter how many times she got burned from learning the unknown, chasing forbidden knowledge, she'd always forgive herself. And she'd never learn.

"I found it, but I can't get it." Cain stepped out from the corner of the room behind MaKayla, thankfully out of sight.

She had known he wasn't going to be able to retrieve her shears. All the carvings, the spells, the enchantments on the old cigar box—they were made specifically to keep someone like Cain Morrigan out.

"And your parents totally have a gun." Cain walked into the room as human and sat at her desk chair. "It's in the safe next to the enchanted box."

"They do?"

"Yep."

MaKayla was surprised, but not shocked. Her Dad was a bit old school, priding himself on being a tough blue-collar guy, but he'd always said there were no guns in the house. Just another parental lie.

"But you said it wouldn't be a problem, that you could get the scissors no problem."

"Listen, this enchantment your mother is toying with is a tremendous power she shouldn't have. I didn't expect her to weave curses so recklessly. I'm constantly wrong for giving humans too much credit."

"I thought Mom and I weren't human."

"Sounds to me like she turned her back on what she was, that she chose to be human."

"That's not fair. You don't understand. You don't know what it's like to not be able to trust your own thoughts, to feel like you're losing control of your own mind to a pair of scissors."

He didn't answer.

"Dad will be working late tomorrow, so I should be able to slip in and get them after school while she's still working in the home office."

"We don't have the time. You need to be snipping heart-strings tomorrow. Besides, we can't leave the safe open and risk them finding it."

"The cigar box is in the gun safe? Where is it in their closet?"

"Behind the plywood square on the wall."

"That was a hole in the wall my brother and I made playing with the closet rods like swords."

"Well, someone used that cut-out as a means to stash a small safe within the wall."

"But that patch is drilled in?"

"Appears so, but it's actually just a magnet. A piece of metal or another magnet should work with a good yank. I'll leave the safe open for you. All you have to do is open the box and retrieve your shears."

"I can't walk by my dad and into his room right now. And I can't creep through their room without waking Mom." MaKayla didn't mention that getting caught could mean getting committed by her own mother.

"Sure, you can. With my help." Cain grinned deviously.

Ivy

His wet, gritty voice kept on. "This is going to be easier than I thought. Please don't misunderstand. I'd always thought this plan impossible, beyond the reach of man. I'd known that, but it satisfied my need for a life's work, one that is a blessing in itself and shall one day be completed. But now...now it's within the realm of possibility. Now I shall take the very last step onto the battlefield against Death. And if it is the same...lickspittle boy I find there, then I shall have him. Let me see the markings of the vessel, girl."

She grabbed the hem of her baggy jeans. They'd been tough to find in local thrift stores, but she couldn't have fabric brushing up against the ever-fresh wounds of the runes.

As inexplicable a change in fashion sense as the wide jeans were, no one would suspect anything from Ivy. She had no problem with abrupt change. She'd played softball with the same group of local girls at the community center since third grade, but as soon as she was allowed to, she quit and never saw half her teammates ever again. She did the same with the middle school AV club and Bible club. So far in high school, she'd ghosted on a D&D campaign, three different language clubs, a church bowling team, and another Bible reading club.

None of these moves were inexplicable to Ivy. Half the decisions to join such clubs were her parent's cyclical attempts to make their kid "normal" after getting frustrated that she was spending too much time with Grandpa, who was getting himself into trouble at his nursing home. The other school organizations she had joined were attempts at research—successful attempts.

She'd written everything she learned in a set of journals, her own collection of holy knowledge so she wouldn't always have to depend on Grandpa's. On top of her own research, she also took down his theories, his ideas that had been deemed the ravings of a sick, old man by his doctors. Grandpa had thousands of snippets from just as many stories filled with occult clues. He spent more time living in old stories than in reality.

In Ivy's mind, though, there was only one story that was important, only one document that took up space in her mind. That was the story of Ivy.

It was a sad tale of a girl more interested in chasing magic than the world around her, a girl and her grandfather forging an undefeatable bond and an ambition no one would understand. In following her passion, her dream, her destiny, she fell victim to ridicule from her parents, Gamma (Grandpa's ex-wife), and countless children at school. But to reach for the stars, to spread oneself out across eternity, to feel the power beyond humanity, Ivy would endure any earthly suffering. And she didn't even consider it suffering. It was white noise, background distraction of people who couldn't see the glory of the universe in motion all around them.

Holy and archaic workings beyond the grasp of mortals interested Ivy, not the clubs and cliques, not the sports teams or political parties. She wore her antisocial demarcation as a badge of honor. Being undependable when it came to the mechanics of high school society wasn't a flaw to Ivy but a feature. Flakiness allowed her to escape from the social burden of high school and withdraw into the monastic life of study she and Grandpa had cultivated. And she'd stare down any number of MaKayla Colfaxes who tried to get too close or who stood in her way.

The runes burning into her flesh were just the physical manifestations of the burdens she carried. Grandpa carried his load on his deathbed, pressing down onto his frail body, the bottom of a crater of cords, cables, and tubes.

The itchiness of the burning runes turned to needling pain as she carefully raised each leg of her jeans. Grandpa licked his lips in anticipation as she went for the gauze.

Everything was moving so fast now. Years had trickled by like well-behaved sand waiting in a single-file line at the top of an hourglass. For so long, she'd fought her own impatience, gathering knowledge, searching for answers, memorizing Grandpa's plans. But now it was here.

Now, Grandpa was ill. New runes burned into her skin every day. Death had visited the hospital room. And Grandpa had driven Death away. Because Grandpa was right. Because she and Grandpa were doing this.

She peeled off the bloody gauze to show Grandpa the runes. They ran up her leg now, searing slashes making up forgotten glyphs.

His bony, pointed finger pressed cold papery skin to the open burns on her calf. Pain stabbed into the burned flesh, and she flinched but forced her leg still as he prodded each symbol. She reminded herself that the pain was good. The pain meant it was working and Grandpa was right.

Then he pinched a rune, and Ivy stifled a cry. Tears escaped her eyes and slid into her mouth. She tried to focus on the taste of salt. Grandpa was only testing her. He had to, to be certain. Because Grandpa was right.

Because she and Grandpa were doing this.

His dull teeth seemed to conceal their brightness in the dim room. His smile was contagious, not like one person causing others to laugh but a madness. Losing one's mind due to the ravings of another.

Ivy smiled. Bright and full of life, awe, and hope. The runes on her flesh burned so good. The taste of salt reminded her it was love and not cruelty.

Cain

It was a simple enough plan...if he could trust MaKayla not to freak out. Humans were awful at such things. And of course, she promised she wouldn't, but Cain found humans were never truly self-aware or honest with themselves. So while MaKayla agreed to the plan to let Cain distract Aaron and hypnotize her mother, he was certain she'd panic and mess things up.

On top of that, the shears themselves, the target of his plan, were such a wildcard. He wasn't able to lift or even move the enchanted box; he might not even be able to touch the scissors.

But he agreed to begin, knowing that this was too much trust to place in a human, but also that he had no choice. He needed a Fate and that meant getting the scissors.

They began.

Cain knocked over an umbrella in the foyer. When little

brother Aaron investigated, Cain knocked a picture frame off the wall in the dining room. Aaron walked across the house and checked the dining room, then Cain set off the security lights in the backyard, leaving the back door open.

The boy was sufficiently spooked, checking the lights in the back while armed with one of his father's golf clubs.

With Aaron out of the way, MaKayla rushed on socked tiptoes down the stairs and across the living room. She slowly turned the knob on the door into her parents' bedroom. She held a breath, pushing the door open with a whispering creak. When it was just barely wide enough, she squeezed through.

Cain's shadow form was much better suited to a darkened room, and he spread himself out in the bedroom of Mr. and Mrs....whatever MaKayla's last name was.

In any case, MaKayla's mom was asleep while Cain acted as a screen, masking all of MaKayla's noise, breath, even her body heat. He watched both women as one snored and the other crept across the carpeted floor in socks.

And then another noise, somewhere in the house.

She froze.

The side door.

MaKayla's dad.

She darted back for the door, but Cain held it closed.

"Let me out!" she whispered in a hiss.

Cain struggled to muffle the sound while holding the door.

Loud footsteps pounded down the hallway.

She shook the doorknob.

Her mom stirred in bed.

"Baby?" Her dad's voice was now on the other side of the door.

MaKayla dashed to hide in the closet.

Feet away, her dad reached for the knob.

Just as Aaron came back inside to tell his dad about hearing things, Cain materialized in the hall bathroom. He made a ruckus, and Dad and Aaron ran for the bathroom.

Empty.

A plate clattered in the kitchen. They scrambled after it, Aaron armed with the golf club. His dad had picked up a melon-sized geode paperweight.

In the creeping shadows, hiding in the peripherals of the two male residents and driving them mad, Cain couldn't keep his mind off the gun in the closet. He had to keep MaKayla's father away from that gun, or MaKayla could wind up dead. He spread himself across the darkness of the house to check the closet, to see how long he had to keep this up.

That's where MaKayla was, holding her breath, walking as silently as possible, blindly searching the closet wall for the plywood patch.

Cain's eyes appeared, bright white coins clear in the blackness.

MaKayla gasped.

Her sleeping mother rustled.

Cain's eyes gestured to the wall, and MaKayla's hands followed until she felt the break in the drywall. She kept one hand on the patch while the other fished the heavy fridge magnet out of her pocket.

As she brought the magnet toward the patch, it leapt from her grasp. The magnet hit the wood with a thud.

"Ray? That you?" her mother moaned groggily.

Meanwhile, across the house, tired of chasing nothings around, MaKayla's dad had had enough. "Room check! One by one. Stay behind me, Aaron, and turn on all lights."

This was bad. As big as MaKayla's house was, they were running out of time.

So Cain hid, descending on Mom, enshrouding her in darkness and silence.

"Ray? Baby?" She reached to the other side of the bed, still half-asleep as Cain absorbed the sound immediately.

But in the closet, MaKayla was panicking. The plywood patch tumbled off the wall. She yipped. She bailed. She ran.

MaKayla

She couldn't do this. Mom or Dad would catch her, and she wouldn't be able to lie. And the truth was now beyond what even Mom would understand. MaKayla would have to admit to unleashing a shadow monster in her own house. Her mom might have her committed. Her dad might have both her and Mom committed. This stupid plan was going to unravel their whole family.

So, she split. Holding her breath, she tip-toe-ran across the soft plush of her parent's bedroom, praying Cain wouldn't be holding the door closed.

"MaKayla," he whispered.

She didn't turn to see him. It was no use anyway in the dark. Even if he left the safe open, the shears were within the box. Even if MaKayla was certain that the box didn't work, it was all the way across the room now.

But then she felt the itch. The unsustainable lack of scissor handles in her hand. Her fingers flexed and closed, grasped at the air for them. She wanted the shears. And not just in her hand—that was just where the yearning started. She wanted those shears back in her possession with every part of her body.

Then she felt the reassuring steel on her fingers.

Impossibly, the scissors had slid into her grasp. Relief and the electricity of excitement coursed through her body, and MaKayla felt herself again.

She opened the door and ducked up the stairs before Dad turned the corner.

Cain was seated at her desk as she walked into her room.

"Do you have them?" he asked, as she shut the door.

She hushed him, livid that he was not taking this as seriously as she was.

"My dad is about to call the cops out there." She imagined strobing police lights as her family was figuratively and literally pulled apart.

"But you got them, right?"

To answer, she gripped the shears behind her back and searched the air in front of Cain. There, anchored to his chest, two translucent cords flowed between gold and navy. What did he call them? Heartstrings. So, with one hand on her shear handles and the other wrapping around Cain's heartstrings, she gave a tug.

He fell from his seat on her desk chair to his knees. But her hope to humble him fell short. He grinned wickedly up at her. "Excellent. Now let's talk about heartstrings."

The straw-colored threads coming from Cain's chest, still in her hand, fell slack. They were so fragile, so delicate, but at the same time strong, like spider silk.

When MaKayla felt the fine thread, she was flooded with emotion—shame, guilt, humiliation. But also, something uneven, like a crush who didn't love you back. There was an intense yearning for acceptance. These emotions overtook her, washing away the immediacy of the threat of her parents, as if their evening of hiding was weeks ago.

Cain lectured like some professor. "Connections between sentient beings manifest themselves. Love is the strongest connection, familial or romantic."

And these were the only feelings she felt, now miles away from any of the cares of her topsy-turvy life. None of that could touch her, there was only the intense emotions of the heartstrings. She looked up from the thread to catch Cain staring at her, then she blushed and turned away.

"But any connection can manifest into a heartstring. Hate, envy, admiration, even debts."

"What about these?" MaKayla held up Cain's two heartstrings, feeling the shame and want coursing through them.

"Familial. These are my parents."

He shook them from her hand and let them go, allowing the heartstrings to pull taut on their own again. The feelings of shame and yearning disappeared as fast as the strings floated back into place.

The emotions the thread conveyed to her suddenly began to make sense. "You have parents?"

"Of course I have parents," he scoffed.

"Okay, fine. I didn't know if you were made out of mud at the dawn of time or something."

"Don't be ridiculous. Nobody was made out of mud at the dawn of..." He trailed off, his eyes looking up and to the side, recalling something. "Well, *I* wasn't made out of mud at the dawn of time. I told you, I'm 17."

"Okay, I didn't know if that was just your human format."

"Form," he corrected her sternly.

But that only goaded her. "And you have multiple forms? Do

I gotta catch them all?"

"Stop."

"I'm sorry."

"Heartstrings can decay on their own time, but they can also be cut short prematurely by supernatural or superhuman forces."

"Like me?"

"Like those shears."

Just as MaKayla was finally starting to get some answers, a knock at the door interrupted them. It was Dad's recognizable knock, three knuckle taps and one slap, but it was aggressive, urgent.

"MaKayla, are you in there?"

"Yeah, Daddy. What's up?"

"Do you want to come out to the living room so we can talk?"

"Um...no?"

"It's important."

"I'm kind of in the middle of something."

"Okay, well...I guess you should know that Mom's going to a hotel. She'll be staying there for a while; we're not sure how long."

The words were an unexpected blow, landing squarely on MaKayla and sending her crashing to the bed in a seated heap. "Okay. Why?"

"She..." He cleared his throat, his quivering voice having a particularly tough time. "She had a gun in the house, baby. So, she'll be at a hotel until we've all had some time to think and talk about what to do next."

"Okay. Can I talk to her?"

Pause.

"She left already, baby."

There were too many emotions to hold in, though MaKayla scrunched every muscle in her face to control the dam-break of feelings. This was all her fault. This was all because of who she was; who she and Mom were. Only MaKayla hadn't listened to her mother. For the first time, her mother had opened up honestly, let her guard down, and MaKayla pushed her away. MaKayla had to go off and figure it out with Mom. And MaKayla, not the police, not the shears of ancient power, but MaKayla had been the one who tore her own family apart.

She flinched at the sensation of someone touching her.

Without looking at her, Cain sat on the floor, one hand on her arm. He just sat there, no expectation of acknowledgment, no expectation at all. That was just where his hand was going to live for a bit.

The simplicity of the gesture devastated her. There was a minute amount of heat passing from his palm, through her tee shirt, and onto her own skin.

Dad spoke again from the other side of the door: "You okay, baby?"

"I guess." Her voice went way too high.

"I love you, baby. We love you. Let me know if you want to talk."

But in the silence that followed, MaKayla didn't want to talk. The connection flowing between her and Cain at that moment was enough to keep her from completely falling apart. They sat like that forever.

Sometime later, when MaKayla had drifted to the gray space between emotionally exhausted and dozing off, Cain's voice, dry and delicate, broke their silence. "We can reschedule for tomorrow night."

"You don't want to lose that much time. I've got library time third and fourth period."

"Okay. I'll see you then. This isn't your fault, you know."

MaKayla's tears turned to venom—Cain just took one step too far. "You don't know me like that. You don't know me well enough to say something like that to me."

She regretted the words as soon as she said them but was powerless to stop speaking. There was a 'yet' missing somewhere in there MaKayla couldn't manage to say. And by the time she thought of apologizing or saying an earnest goodbye to make some peace, he was already gone.

Chapter 7

Cain

Hospitals didn't sleep like other buildings slept. There was no blanket darkening of windows, and the smattering of lights was inconsistent. The building was awake with movement, perhaps a little drowsy compared to the daytime scurry of activity. This building was alive, if barely. Figures moved, but slowly. Lights were dull. In some windows, color danced from screens.

Cain knew exactly which window was Grandpa Skelton's. The hollow window eyes stared dully out into the night, unfocused. But like the old man, it was a ruse; he was playing possum. The room was brimming with razor-sharp focus. Things were never as they seemed.

Like MaKayla. She'd been through more in one night than anyone Cain knew, certainly more than any of the other kids at school. She always seemed so together; the persona she put out into Seville High School society was very near-perfect, this flawless being effortlessly excelling in all subjects plus popularity and somehow having this wellspring of depth expressed through art. And all in a perfect package. MaKayla was as beautiful and put-together as any of the most popular girls in school, which, yeah, made her appear shallow and perhaps a little less intelligent in day-to-day discourse, but that was a lie. A meat-eating plant disguised as a flower.

And hadn't he tried the same thing, hitting on her as some mindless chauvinistic bro? Only he couldn't pull it off. MaKayla pulled it off every day.

His phone buzzed.

There was a delicious point in time as he reached for the phone where the message awaiting him was Schrodinger's text: it was simultaneously the greatest message imaginable and the worst news possible from MaKayla.

He imagined a confession; an admission of feelings, longing, lustful teenage thoughts from MaKayla, but also the saddest news possible, a turn for the worse for her mother and father's relationship, or maybe even an incident that would involve culling the soul of MaKayla's mother.

But the text was from his own mother, checking in.

"*You know I can help get this assignment on time without involving your father.*"

He typed out a response, "*I can do this. Why don't you believe in me?*" but deleted it instead of sending it.

Instead of being angry with his mom's lack of confidence in him, which he'd always suspected was there, he couldn't stop thinking about MaKayla and the texts Cain had been expecting to get from her.

What was Cain expecting? Especially the state he left her in just a couple hours ago? Something romantic? Sexual? That hadn't been their relationship. Nothing physical had come up at all.

But then he thought about putting his hand on her arm, the softness of her shoulder. He remembered the firm tug she gave to his own heartstring, showing her strength. The deliciously bilious look she threw at him as he was hitting on her with Chad-like machismo.

This was ridiculous. He was being ridiculous. He needed MaKayla to snip whatever powerful heartstring was anchoring Grandpa Skelton. That was it. Soon, he'd be saying goodbye to Seville High School and his fleshy human form forever. Hopefully.

Mom texted again. "*Please don't stay out all night.*"

MaKayla was just a means to an end. A tool he required for a project. He needed to think of her that way, not with any sticky, gooey human attachments. Clinical. Use her and say goodbye.

The lie that he was there to train her would help. He'd scour the library for any other tidbits about Fates, maybe even do some googling.

By tomorrow, he'd have an entire spiel fit for a mentor of Fates. A good lie, a nice big one wedged between them so they couldn't get closer. It was safer that way. For both of them.

Still, the very human thoughts of what MaKayla *could* have been texting him gnawed at his mind.

MaKayla

MaKayla had reserved so many study rooms at the library, whether it was for clubs, art projects, or group assignments, she understood the system all too easily. Cain wandered around the bulletin board of sign-in sheets like a foreigner in a busy bus station.

As he suggested, MaKayla found the most central study room available in the library, which was nearly all glass on two sides up two stories, filling the aisles and shelves with natural light.

All of the study rooms had glass window walls as well, so as soon as they got in, Cain set about closing the blinds. MaKayla had a seat at the far end of a conference table, watching a taut loveline cut through the room.

"Is everything okay? With your family."

"We're not here to talk about that."

"Okay then." After closing the final set of blinds, Cain locked the door and dropped his voice. "The Fates were the daughters of gods, some say of Nyx, goddess of night, but others think—"

"Zeus, right. I have the same internet as you."

"Yes, well. One sister was said to have spun the very thread of life, another to measure its appropriate length, and the last—"

"To cut it," she interrupted. "Clotho, Lachesis, and Atropos. Can we skip the basic run down and explain how this actually works?"

"I'm trying. The gods, even those who birthed the sisters, feared their powers."

'Yeah, but what *are* the powers? And where did I get them from? And my mom is another Fate; I don't have a sister."

"I'll get to that."

She was so sick of being kept in the dark, of not knowing. Not knowing about her lineage from her mom, then the knowledge withheld about her powers from Cain. And on top of those, she was in the dark about the fate of her own family. Well she was finished pretending it was okay. MaKayla was done being kept at arm's length from the truth. she lashed out at Cain.

"Will you? Because so far, you've only told me stuff that I've already found with a basic internet search. Meanwhile, I don't know anything more about me, or what's happening, or anything about you besides the fact you can turn into a mysterious shadow monster!"

"You're immortal." The words landed like a slap in the face, leaving her dazed and woozy, her view of the world as shaky as her now-clumsy footing.

"What? That's not possible. My grandma died..."

"Immortal...as long as you hold the shears or are in contact with them."

Mom had claimed that her mother had told her as much, but it was dismissed as the ravings of a crazy woman.

"You're telling me my grandmother willingly let go of them? Knowing she'd die? Or were they kept from her all these years, and she died naturally as a human? Did she even have a choice?"

"I didn't know your grandmother, MaKayla. I do know that *you* have a choice. Every day of your existence, you will have a choice whether or not to pick up those shears or leave them and this part of yourself behind you. If you do, you will live your human life. If you don't, if you always choose the shears, you will live forever."

"And always be haunted by these thoughts?" She glared at the loveline cutting through the room, taunting her.

"Thoughts? The shears have communicated with you? What are these thoughts?"

"I was hoping you'd tell me. I can't stop thinking about Ora and Mark. You don't know anything about these thoughts or how to control them?"

"Of course I do. I'm... just surprised you've been... communing with your scissors so soon. When did you say you got them?"

"Three days ago."

"Yeah…" he seemed to be stalling or stumbling for an answer. "Communing can take weeks. Seems like you're a natural."

"So how do I make them stop?"

"I don't know if they ever truly stop. But you can learn to control them *if* you listen to me and do as I say."

Great. Again this dude wanted obedience, subservience. But if she had to ignore the grosser parts of his mentorship, she would.

"Okay, so what do I do?" she asked.

"What do you know so far?"

"Next to nothing. I didn't know my grandmother was still alive until she died and left me these. They came with my name engraved on them. They…want to be held. And my hands want to hold them. My body desires to hold them. And when I do, I see the connections between people, the wires."

"The heartstrings."

"Sure."

"Or lovelines."

"Whatever you say." She approached the heartstring running through the library study room. She could reach out and grasp it, just as easily as she could wave her hand through it. "I see them, and if I focus, I can touch them. But if I don't focus—"

"They pass right through you."

Okay…so this guy did know his stuff.

"That's right."

"That's because lovelines don't exist within our dimension in a physical state. Here, they're made of psychic, emotional energy. But on other planes, these energies manifest physically."

"Then how can I touch them? I can hold them in my hand,

and I... feel their connection. Their relationship. I relive all the moments from each of their eyes all at once."

"'How' makes for difficult questions. The 'how' might be a very scientific explanation about the exchange of energies or transitions between physical planes. The 'how' also might be because Zeus bedded a Greek lady."

"Bedded?"

Again, Cain blushed. He quickly went on, "The why is more important than the how. It's essential you know why you do what you're doing, and that lies with you. But knowing what you're doing- I aim to help with that. We'll get started in a second; in the meantime, focus your breathing and be aware of the lovelines around the room as we talk. Now tell me about communing with the shears."

"Well, the first heartline—"

"Heartstring," he corrected.

"The first heartstring I could see clearly was between Mark and Ora. this one," she gestured to the thread running through the room. "That was three days ago, and I keep thinking about them., whether I'm near their loveline or not."

"Ora, the girl—"

"Aurora. Only I call her Ora. Works with me at the art store. My best friend. She's freaking out because she thinks he's cheating, and they've both been miserable in this relationship, but they think they're destined to be together. And I just want to..." MaKayla trailed off, focused on the taut thread running through the study room.

"What?"

"I want to cut their loveline. I *need* to. It's...it's the most intrusive thought besides wanting to hold the shears."

"Good. That's good. Must be your first assignment."

"First assignment?" An odd warm hope spread across MaKayla's tired body. A glimmer of action she could take to advance her cause— something she could control. If there was one thing MaKayla Colfax could do, it was complete an assignment. She'd been doing it for years with aplomb.

"So, I'll cut it!" She reached for the loveline and brought the open mouth of her shears up.

"Wait." His words froze her. "If you truly want to break free of these intrusive thoughts and gain control of your power, you'll need to exercise that muscle. Spend some time ignoring the assignment—"

"I told you; I've been ignoring it for days and can't stop thinking—"

"Then ignore it a little longer. Cut when *you* decide. Control the shears, or the shears will control you. Then, for the following assignment, delay a little longer, maybe cut an unassigned heartstring first. Build up your resistance. Strengthen your control."

"An unassigned heartstring? I could just *decide* to cut a heartstring? Just 'snip' two people apart? What would happen? Would they break up or just...forget about each other?

It was suddenly a very sad thought. Her finger ran along Ora and Mark's graying thread, and she felt the angst within it. Of course, she *wanted* to snip it, but what then? Go on to the next couple to break up? But that's what her destiny was, wasn't it? Severing ties between people? Breaking up couples and families? Heartbreak? An eternity of spreading sorrow? Unless...

"Will I ever be assigned to snip someone's life?"

He laughed at the idea. "What? Like a Reaper?"

When she didn't laugh with him, Cain cleared his throat and

changed expressions. Through a razor-ship Cheshire smile, he said greasily, "A Fate would need to become incredibly powerful to do the work of a Reaper."

What was this world he was revealing to her? Gods and Fates and Reapers? What kinds of monsters were out there besides Cain himself? What kind of monster would she become?

"How would I choose?" she asked herself quietly, before pointing out, "I can see the problems Mark and Ora are having. I can feel their jealousy, frustration, anger, fear, and...oh my God."

"What do you feel?"

"Infidelity. It's... She's wrong, it's not a girl from another school. It's hazy, but it's there. Feelings. Desire. A kiss, but maybe a dream. It feels like kissing someone. It's...it's Ivy Skelton."

"Ivy Skelton? Mark Cecilia is cheating on Aurora with Ivy Skelton? Is Ivy even capable of real feelings?"

"Everyone is capable of real feelings. Even you."

"Don't insult me," Cain said. "And don't get too caught up in the drama. This isn't a TV show to watch and choose your favorite characters. It's a job. A sacred charge."

"To split people up."

"For everyone's benefit. What would happen if you were still hung up on your first crush? What if you continued to develop feelings for a celebrity even when you found out they were a horrible person? What if you were expected to maintain every single positive connection you'd ever had?"

"I'd be exhausted all the time."

"Exactly."

"Which I am already."

"This is maintenance. Controlled burns to enrich the soil."

"These are people, Cain."

"Exactly. Stop thinking of them as these great heroic figures. They're dirty, stinking humans, each in the absolute center of their own universe. We do not have that luxury. We have to see the complicated universe as it is: ineffable, untamable, and cold."

"Someone's cold."

"Fine. Homework: think about how Aurora and Mark's life would be if they never break up. Put some thought into it. Let me know how their lives would look."

"Easy. Not healthy."

"Beyond that. How does the emotional weight of a decaying heartstring affect one's GPA? What kind of career does one get when one stays connected beyond reason? Second part of homework: find another couple who needs breaking up. Not a loveline you are attracted to, not something your shears communicate to; go out, touch some heartstrings, look deep into the relationships, and find a pair who are better off without one another."

"I don't think that's for me to decide."

He dropped his voice to low, slow, and overly spooky. "It's imperative that we discern whether you're powerful enough to sever an unassigned loveline."

She again felt she was on the precipice of something exciting and scary. Her life, her world, would never be the same again. And this guy, this seemingly normal, kind of cute goth boy was her only source of knowledge—no other books, sites, teachers, or resources. Just him. And there was obviously a huge well of experience and learning behind his gorgeous gray eyes. She just couldn't get past his gross attitude.

"I can't believe you're giving me homework."

"Fine then, no homework. Can you...when can you meet me at Seville Cemetery?" Again, he just insisted.

"I can't tonight. I have inventory, and I won't get out until midnight."

"We'll meet then."

This guy was the worst.

She seethed fake enthusiasm through clenched teeth. "Great. I'll see you then."

But it had actually gone well. He did know his stuff, and she would learn to control and ignore this power of hers.

And while Cain untwisted all the blinds back open, MaKayla walked out of the study room and right into Ora.

Cain

It all had gone horribly wrong.

Cain was stumbling for answers, on the defensive the entire time. He made up half the stuff he told her and would immediately have to commit these lies to writing so he could keep up the facade. And he'd failed in instilling any sense of urgency in her. She felt no rush in severing an unassigned loveline, but if he was to harvest the soul on time, she absolutely had to.

So he set to writing everything from that conversation down in the back of his English notebook before he forgot. But while he was trying to keep straight everything he told MaKayla, he noticed her outside the study room window.

She hadn't gone to her next class. She had run into Aurora. Just the person he didn't want her spending too much time with. If MaKayla was unable to snip a heartstring that she wasn't assigned, she would be useless to Cain and his assignment.

Unless...

Unless he could teach her how to read the heartstrings better. Maybe that would help. She could touch Grandpa Skelton's enchanted heartstring, read into it, and see why it's so powerful.

Momentarily, Cain coveted MaKayla's powers, her ability to reach and touch these lovelines, these inter dimensional bonds, and understand these humans and their motives. Instead, he lived in a world unknowable to humans. Except MaKayla.

He made notes of all the things he said were true, but he actually had no idea.

Three days, communing with shears—quick for a Fate

Only sees heartstrings/lovelines while holding shears (like immortality)

Telepathy into memories of relationship only when touching lovelines—requires focus

Desire to hold shears, desire to cut specific loveline as assignment

He thought he'd finished making note of everything when the room suddenly went cold.

Or maybe that was just that Cain noticed who walked in.

Ivy Skelton, untucked, unmade-up, bereft of any damns to give, stood awkwardly in the study room, looking at the USA-centric map poster on the wall. And as if they were in the middle of a longer conversation, she said, "Anyway, so my grandad is super abusive towards me, but he was all the family I had for a while, and so we're close, and it's weird and complicated and ugly, but he's dying, and so I've been a real bitch lately. And I wanted to say sorry to the people I've been taking it out on."

Her brown-in-blue eyes flashed up, locking with Cain's for a moment.

The look bore into Cain, iced his joints, and froze his thoughts.

His jaw tightened, then his throat and chest, then the rest of him.

She said in a whiny whisper, like a painful secret. "I'm sorry, Cain."

Her words and legs trembled, then she rushed out of the room and library.

In her wake, the oversized glowing golden loveline trailed behind, leading across town to her grandpa's hospital room.

Cain stifled an immediate desire to run after her. Such a disgusting human impulse, to attend to one another's emotions. From his limited observations, only that person can really heal themselves mentally but rarely did they.

That was twice now he'd reached out with that very intent of helping a human in emotional pain, once seeing MaKayla react to her parent's fight and now suppressing a rush to comfort Ivy Skelton.

Hopefully, Cain was simply understanding humans better, as his mom had always wanted. Hopefully, he was not letting his guard down and slipping.

He closed the door to the study room and reviewed his notes, filling the margins with recollections and theories.

MaKayla

According to the memories MaKayla had been experiencing, Mark wasn't just hooking up with Ivy; he was in love with her. Images of leaning in to kiss her interrupted more and more of the memories of Mark and Ora together. And it was getting worse as the day went on. Then came the thirst.

MaKayla had never felt anything like it—not just looking into a memory, experiencing it, this was someone else's feelings overtaking her own. When she touched their heartstring, MaKayla wanted to drink. Not just drink but get drunk. Wasted. In fact, she wanted drugs, too. Pills, weed, anything.

But then she'd lose contact with the heartstring, and the compulsion, the thirst, would fade. But then she'd want it back, her mind would drift, and she'd find herself reaching with one hand for her shears and the other for Ora's heartstring.

That's how most of the night counting inventory at the art supply store went. Instead of being the diligent work-first employee she usually was, MaKayla was chatty, following Ora around all night, touching and grasping the heartstring as often and as inconspicuously as possible.

She was caught once or twice, mostly blaming stray hairs, complaining about shedding, new shampoo, or her sweater's ability to collect lint.

Her distracted and delayed work led to getting out late, but she had plenty of intel on Mark and Ora's connection. Spending time holding the string, thinking her way through the memories and feelings, sifting through the relationship, was a skill MaKayla now had to develop. Like navigating a library's network or learning a museum website's search interface, she needed to learn how to parse out and find specific items. Otherwise, it was a rush of too much information at once. A data tsunami.

So, she had mentally prepared herself to develop her skills as her headlights rolled across the stone and iron perimeter of Seville Cemetery and landed on the stark white-on-black figure of Cain Morrigan. He flinched from the bright light, looking so vampiric he may have hissed.

This guy.

Honestly, if MaKayla knew that monsters were real and hiding in plain sight in her school, Cain Morrigan would have been the first person she'd suspect. First off, his name was Cain Morrigan. Secondly, he was a known loner. He wore all black. Like literally nothing but black shirts covered by black coats above black jeans down to black boots over black socks. Plus, he was antisocial. Not just avoiding making friends or joining any extracurriculars, he obviously thought he was better than everybody else. At assemblies, if he even bothered to show up, he'd sit in back and sneer, read, or sleep.

And now he'd convinced MaKayla to hang out with him in a cemetery after midnight. She parked and killed the lights, taking time to bundle up against the dropping cold, shooting a text to her dad that she was grabbing a hot cocoa with a coworker before heading home. They'd let it slide that she didn't come right home after work. MaKayla had built up over sixteen years of goodwill by being a good girl and not breaking the rules.

The cemetery was well-kept, with matching trees dotting the fencing at exact intervals.

"I want to cut the Ora/Mark loveline as soon as possible. Tonight, if we can."

"Good evening to you as well. Tonight's lesson will be about feeling the differences between different lovelines."

"Did you not hear me? I need to cut Mark out of Ora's life right now."

"I've told you: not until you sever an unassigned connection."

"And I told you, it's not for me to decide."

"Which brings me to tonight's lesson: sensing the difference between connections. There are lots of connections anchored here, mostly people who visit their loved ones and speak to the gravestones. Humans hold onto feelings. Not just love. Grudges, too. Focusing on heartstrings without touching them, can you see any differences?"

At first, it was like squinting. Then relaxing her eyes. Then crossing them. Finally, she simply looked harder, focusing on one thread, on one point. Moonlight danced as if the loveline were a spider's web, thin and delicate gossamer.

Another loveline running from the same grave was thicker, heavier with a slight dip. This yarn was a dull mustard, rustic with inconsistent threads unwinding and fraying.

The thin spider silk line was pure, simple. The idea of a person. A thin connection of people without baggage. MaKayla understood intuitively, like Cain had practically dared her to. She also knew the rustic mustard yarn was a historied connection, millions of fibrous memories spun into connective tissue of the inter dimensional relationship of two people.

"You're right; there are differences." MaKayla no longer needed her flashlight to see the sprouting lovelines bunched together at random graves.

She paused at one as Cain slowly made his way around, signaling with his light beam, pointing out each marker. "Surgeon, minister, teacher, librarian, teacher, surgeon. So much love for surgeons. Very few heartstrings going out to general practitioners. None for the dentists or any other people helped in that surgery. God knows nurses do all the work. Whoever gave the right anesthesia also saved a life…"

"Coach." The title was at the front of the gravestone's name. Lovelines flew out from the headstone like drops of water flying from a splashed puddle. Threads of all colors and thicknesses strewn out from the marker towards town.

According to the tombstone, he was a high school coach, baseball and softball. Many of these lovelines were matching, appearing a shimmering brass the width of twine, all tightly wound, no fibrous flyaways. Without touching, MaKayla could feel the connections; she sensed the type of relationships were there, all alike—a coach, a mentor, a hero, an ideal of masculinity and leadership, sharing memories of victories and failure, fetishizing pain and struggle, worshiping the stoic. The only emotions were pain and victory.

These were his players, the young people he helped mold into the adults of the community they were today.

But some lovelines didn't match the other players. Some weren't shimmering copper, but rather orange-hued; a rusted cord, not straight or drooping but full of crooked kinks and awkward angles. At first, these cords simply caught MaKayla's eye, but soon, they communicated much, much more. Simply staring at the loveline, she felt it: fear. Shame. Disgust at oneself, driving a silent agony of guilt which only increased the disgust. Hatred and self-hatred.

"These were his victims."

Cain looked at MaKayla, not the rusted cords. "Not all the connections are based on love."

The threads were within reach for MaKayla. An insatiable curiosity made her want to feel the heartstring in her own hand, to feel the depth of pain, to grasp that rotten connection. But from this distance, she felt so much, so deeply; she paused. Did she want more of these sensations? Did she want to feel the cold, hollow shame coursing through her mind? Her hand froze midway to the rusted cord.

"These are the connections you have the power to sever. On the other end of these connections are souls, still alive, who can't let go of this pain."

The hatred within the rusted cords was soon her own. Who was this coach, and how dare he do this to so many, make them feel small, meaningless, no more than game pieces for a man, and authority figure, to control and use?

How deep was their trauma? What had this coach done?

Yes, she could cut the cords. And presumably, Cain was right; she could release living souls. But that meant touching the rusted cords, tainting her own mind with this evil, infecting herself with the fear and pain she'd be freeing others from.

"Who am I to do this to other people? This power is wrong."

"This power is yours. And it's only the beginning. If you can learn to control it, your powers, your responsibilities, will go much further than heartstrings. You're a Fate, MaKayla, you can…"

"Kill? Is that what all of this is leading me to? Grow powerful enough to choose who lives and dies?"

"We are not simple humans, MaKayla. Our existence isn't predicated on money, class, taxes, popularity. Ours is an existence above. It may be difficult to see now, but…we are something more."

"Then why do we still have these?" MaKayla gestured to the strings reaching out from her own heart, two going to her father and brother back home, one veering in another direction toward her mother in a nearby hotel.

Without even thinking, she motioned to the two strings going out from Cain's chest, her fingertips brushing against it.

Instantly she was hit with emotion—embarrassment, self-reproach, powerlessness. Suddenly, MaKayla felt not good enough for anything; she was no longer split about being a Fate, but rather felt incompetent, not good enough to be a Fate, never able to measure up to this standard of her bloodline. But the emotions weren't hers—they were held within the connection between Cain and one of his parents. She'd only been in contact for a moment, but the power of the helplessness took over her mind, then vanished as soon as her contact with the loveline ceased. The self-reproach ebbed away, leaving an empty pit in her thoughts where insurmountable self-doubt had been.

"Is that your mother?" MaKayla couldn't remove her eyes from the thread stretching from Cain's chest, a fiery red frayed cord.

"Don't." He walked away.

"So, it's fair game as long as they're human, but for some reason, you're above it all?"

"*We!*" he sneered. "We're above it! I do not understand your insistence on holding on to your humanity. It's unflattering and ignorant."

"I don't know why the concept of being human is so despicable to you, but you're a person, too. Even if you're not a human, you're a person. With thoughts and feelings and terrible fashion sense, and your connections are with other people. Even if they're not human. And I felt in that connection that there's someone who's making you feel like you're not good enough, like you're less than what you're supposed to be. I think that's why you point at your humanity like it's a flaw. And that's why you condescend to me every time you open your mouth. Well, I won't be condescended to, and I'm not going to listen to someone tell me that loving other people is ignorant or unflattering. If that's all you have to teach, then I don't need it. I'll find someone else."

"There is no one else."

"Then I won't learn." And with that, she turned to head back to her car.

"MaKayla, wait." He slumped to lean against an obelisk, his pale skin and gaunt features fitting in well with the graveyard. He smiled. "I thought I had great fashion sense."

She ended her exit for the car and folded her arms. "You wear all black every day."

"Wearing black is cool."

"It can be. But you wear it like you're hiding."

"I figured it was neutral, goes with anything."

"Nothing is neutral," she said.

"I don't mean to talk down to you. This is just...this is all very new to me."

"Weird. That almost sounds like the truth. You've never trained a Fate before?"

She knew it was true. This guy knew a lot, but he stumbled over any direct Fate-centric questions.

"No."

"Good. Now that we both know that neither of us knows what we're doing, we can move forward. I'll keep looking for connections that are better off severed."

"So we can keep training?"

"I guess so. You're still the person who knows the most about all of this."

"And you'll sever an unassigned cord?"

She sighed and answered, convincing herself more than him. "Yes."

"Besides the coach's victims?"

"We don't know what would happen if I suddenly cut those connections. It might not heal them; it might create more turmoil. I'll keep looking. I'm working all weekend, but I can see you on Sunday night."

"Why not tomorrow?"

"Why are you in such a hurry? Is there something you're not telling me?"

"No."

She didn't believe that.

"Well, when you decide to admit that's a lie, you can call me, and we can rearrange our schedules. Otherwise, I can meet you at your place Sunday night."

Behind the mask of darkness, hiding behind his beam of light, Cain pouted over MaKayla's stubbornness. But he soon found out what most people who knew MaKayla and her mom found out – trying to win wasn't worth the fight.

"I work Sunday night."

"You work?" The thought was so out-of-character for him. She immediately pictured him dressed in corporate gear for a fast-food franchise, and the visual was utterly ridiculous. "Where do you work?"

"Here." He looked down and kicked at the rocks.

That made more sense. Cain absolutely fit in at the cemetery. Like MaKayla fit in at school...only not anymore. Just going to school, pretending to be a normal student, interacting with her friends was too difficult of a task for her. "I can't keep lying like this. I'm no good at it, and I don't want to. I know Mark is cheating; I need to say something to her."

"Listen, I'm trying to be diplomatic about this. You... interfere with this relationship—isn't that crossing an ethical line?"

"She's my friend. If I know something, I should say something."

"Fine. Do what you will. But she's gonna start asking questions. The kind of questions that force answers, like, 'I'm an immortal Fate.' And 'I inherited telepathic scissors.' So I hope Aurora is understanding."

She could have cursed him, but Cain was annoyingly right. He seemed to always be so wrong about people, about the substance of relationships and the goodness in people, and then he'd be one hundred percent correct on everything else. He was so frustrating.

Cain

Dear gods, Cain was lucky he was so good at lying. He'd never admit that MaKayla was smarter than him, but she pushed back against every lie he told as if she could see right through him.

This was why he didn't like humans. They were so stubborn, so hell-bent on understanding things, even in the face of the expansive and unknowable. And MaKayla wasn't even human. Not anymore, anyway. Not with those scissors living in her grasp as they were. She probably didn't even notice them in her hand anymore, but Cain noticed.

She was changing, becoming something new. Cain couldn't play this wrong. He had to keep encouraging her to learn and control her powers. But even he had to admit he had no idea what her powers would end up being. Especially if he pushed her. She could end up more powerful than Cain...for now. But he had his parents around if things got out of hand, but only if he absolutely had to. And there was no way a Fate could be more powerful than two angels of Death...right?

He chewed his lip and tapped the steering wheel in the greenish light of his dashboard. Through binoculars, he had a clear view into the Skelton hospital room windows, but it

113

obstructed his deeper vision. Through man-made lenses, it was more difficult to study the abundance of ties festooning out from the corner of the cubic building.

If he focused, concentrated on one tie, like the drooping rope, he could make it out, barely, through the binoculars, but it would be blurry or incomplete. He wondered if MaKayla would be able to see through lenses better than him. It was worth trying. Just to get more surveillance on the old man.

But he had to watch himself around her. She read into his relationship with his parents. She could wind up exposing them all.

Then he would be in real trouble.

But MaKayla Colfax *was* trouble. He knew it the moment he saw her following invisible lovelines down the hallway. He may have known it before that. MaKayla stood out in the crowd. She was one of the beautiful girls, but she didn't hang out with them. Cain imagined she did well in school; she was smart and did plenty of extracurriculars.

And he was already thinking too much about her. This was about culling a soul. Soon enough, he'd be a Reaper, and frivolous high school dramas would be far behind him.

Suddenly, there was movement in Skelton's hospital room. The curtains parted and swept back to reveal a short figure.

The binoculars showed Ivy Skelton's curvy figure, reaching up, revealing her midriff and bottom of her bra to Cain, and his body reacted. He sucked in a breath, his skin clammy. Boxers tightening. Pits wet and sour with nervous sweat. She aggravated his male teenage form, and he was too busy to mind it.

She was trouble, too. Ivy was classic trouble, though; she skipped more classes than Cain and was almost never without a crew, which seemed to change every couple of months, whether it was the band kids, the D&D kids, the comic book nerds, or the other random goth stragglers. But when she'd cornered him in the library today, she'd been alone. In fact, she'd been alone a lot lately, as far as Cain could remember.

And why the confession? Was Ivy really feeling guilty about her run-in with Cain? something about it felt...wrong. Not that she was lying; what she said felt genuine. But why was she saying it to him? Why would Ivy open up like that?

It hit him suddenly. Did Ivy Skelton have a crush on Cain? He'd never had to navigate that aspect of teenage society and he was out of his depth in any attempt to decipher the clues. Was he just imagining things? Wasn't Ivy having some sort of tryst with Ora's boyfriend?

The idea of Mark Cecilia putting his neanderthal hands on Ivy disgusted Cain and soured his mood. Fine. He'd find out. He could roll his eyes and stomp about, but deep down, Cain wanted to know for himself: could a guy like Mark Cecilia really just wind up with whomever he pleased?

Meanwhile, in the Skelton hospital room, the curtains fell back into place, and the room was again vaguely yellow. Ivy was gone, leaving a sheet of paper taped up with a single word on it.

"Hi."

Ivy

This couldn't be right.

Grandpa said there were no such things as coincidences, and as always, he was right. She was really getting tired of that.

It wasn't always this way; Grandpa's theories had always been theories, long shots, and feeble attempts at knowing the unknowable. But recently, just as she was getting ready to say goodbye to him for good, everything he had ever told her was winding up correct.

He was going to defeat Death. With her.

And they would become more powerful than they ever imagined, just like he said.

But he also said that the Death they sent for him was a lickspittle, an underling, sent to do the job. He'd guessed that this angel of Death was a boy, maybe even a boy in her school.

So just in case, Ivy brought a yearbook for him to peruse. At first, Grandpa didn't find "that damn Lickspittle" among any of the class pictures.

But on another page, among the candid photos taken around school, a picture was circled in red ink. There was a student in the background of an assembly, walking away. A student who didn't have his personal photo in with the rest of his class. Probably skipped it. This outcast, too good for posed photos, too good for assemblies, this was the boy Grandpa claimed was Lickspittle.

That damn warlock boy, Cain Morrigan.

Everything changed at that moment. These weren't hypothetical situations she was reading in ancient texts. This wasn't the a collection of natural elements governing reality. This was her life. And somehow, one of her classmates was a reality-governing element.

She tried to warn Cain, to tell him to stay away without giving anything away, but her guilt got the best of her. If Cain Morrigan really was some form of walking Death, she no longer felt so ambitious or thirsty for immortal knowledge. She just felt sorry for the guy in her class.

She didn't like Grandpa being right anymore. It was no longer a thrill but a gnawing dread. What other dark claims of his would she find out were true?

Chapter 8

MaKayla

Ora was super short with MaKayla at work as they unboxed and built display shelves. Then suddenly, she blurted, "I think I'm going to quit the store and go work for my dad."

That made absolutely no sense. "As an electrician? Isn't that like years of training and certification?"

"Working in the office," Ora sneered, like MaKayla was an idiot. "They need help nights and weekends. And the last girl that did filings and phones for them just got promoted to full time, and now she makes bank."

"How could you work a full-time job and go to Seville?"

"It's just a part-time job for now. It'd only be full-time if they really liked me and wanted to hire me on."

"What, instead of going to college?"

"I don't know. Maybe."

But Ora had a dream and a plan that she'd been over with MaKayla thousands of times. "That's ridiculous. What about design school? What about making art books and designing children's books?"

"I can still do that if I want."

"Will you be able to work nights with cheering and yearbook staff?"

"I quit."

Ora was being so unlike herself MaKayla was having difficulty following. "You quit? Which?"

"Both." She chuckled. Like it was funny.

"What? You love yearbook. And cheering. Why?"

"Jesus, why are you being so annoying about this? You sound like my mom. Just because I'm good at the yearbook software and can memorize cheers doesn't mean that's my life, okay? It's just stupid high school stuff anyway."

This was so unlike her best friend. MaKayla was reeling. "Ora, we're in high school. We're supposed to do high school stuff. And you'd never call the yearbook stupid."

"Well, it is. It's just a group of students picking the best pictures of their best friends—it's all so shallow and vain and stupid. Really, I felt better the moment I quit."

The words hung in the air for a moment, then MaKayla said carefully, like defusing a bomb, trying not to set her friend off again, "Ora, do you think you're just upset about Mark, and that's leading you to make these decisions?"

"I don't know why you're so obsessed with me and Mark. Me and Mark are fine. Real couples have ups and downs—they don't just give up if things are tough. You'd know that if you had a boyfriend, or girlfriend, or whatever."

That one hurt. Ora had been the one to listen to MaKayla when her crushes didn't reciprocate. She'd been the one to comfort MaKayla and insist nothing was wrong with her. She felt tears threaten as she asked, "Why are you being like this?"

"Like what?"

"Look." MaKayla took a breath and held it together. "If you don't want to talk, that's fine. We won't talk. And if you quit the store, I will miss you so, so much, and we'll just have to plan a big night to celebrate you moving onto bigger and better things."

"Plans are for fools."

"Excuse me?"

"Man plans, God laughs. You can plan all you want, MaKayla, but if you're destined to do something, or be with someone, or be at a particular place at a particular time, God or the universe or whatever will put you there. You can plan until you're blue in the face. Doesn't stop people from being who they are, getting their jobs or quitting extracurriculars, or moving out."

That last sentence was a gut-punch. She had to sever this connection Ora had with Mark before Ora threw her whole future away.

Cain

Cain was not looking forward to today. Not just as another day in the super-purgatory known as American high school, but he was supposed to socialize. With Mark Cecilia.

There was a special kind of ritual Cain felt left out of; social norms of which he was ignorant. He would say the wrong thing and insult the guy. Or worse, his approach would wind up so laughable, Mark wouldn't even slow down to talk.

But part of Cain was quite curious about how a guy like Mark could not only date a girl like Aurora but also manage to hook up with someone like Ivy Skelton. Granted, humans were curiously erratic and fickle, but Cain thought he'd developed some perspective of the high school social ecosystem.

Cain tugged at the collar of his shirt. He had opted for a plaid shirt in navy blue, gray, and red, though it was mostly navy blue and gray, thankfully. Cain thought it was way too much color, even with black jeans, his black bracelets, and black boots. Mom had proven as much, commenting on how great it looked. Why had he dressed like this? He was probably self-conscious from what MaKayla said, plus he had anxiety about fitting in with a fellow normal teenage guy.

As if he were some fool, Cain was early to school, timing a chance meeting with Mark, who should be finishing a before-school workout, or practice, or whatever jock ritual this time of year called for. But what would Cain say? He'd already failed miserably with MaKayla when he tried going undercover as a normal student. What could a social pariah like Cain possibly say to a jock like Mark?

Cain calmed himself, wiping his hands on his black jeans, settling down with every breath.

In the pre-homeroom chaos of the halls, Cain focused on Mark, changing out books at his locker, slapping hands.

Over and over, Cain reminded himself what he'd learned from MaKayla: everyone at Seville High School thought he was a maniac, or at least mentally unwell. Cain would use this to his advantage. He pounded the rest of his coffee and slung it into a trashcan, put on his meanest mug, and marched up to the popular jock.

"What's up, Mark?" Cain managed his most threatening voice, spitting the words in menacing disgust. While not physically imposing, Cain knew others probably figured he was armed. Nobody at school knew his family; for all anyone knew, his family was way into guns.

Cain opened his eyes wide, allowing a caffeine-induced twitch to spasm in the corner of one eye.

He set his dead, threatening stare at Mark and awaited his off-put jelly-kneed reaction. A monster with a soft and goopy human in the palm of his hand.

But Mark didn't miss a beat. "Oh, hey man. What you got?"

"What do I what?"

Mark was barely even noticing the dangerous face Cain had practiced all morning. The jock didn't look up from a struggle to fit his books into his bag, his hands working clumsily and his eyes glassy.

Wait, was this guy drunk?

"I don't need Ambien or Ritalin, but I could use some Molly."

"Molly?" Cain didn't know any Seville student by that name, although it was popular enough... Wait. Cain knew what this was. "You think I'm a drug dealer?"

Mark's glassy gaze suddenly made lots of sense.

"Fine, whatever, no drugs. What you got? Vodka? Weed?"

"Weed and alcohol are drugs."

"Whoa. *you* came up to *me*, man," Mark said.

"Oh...yeah."

"So?"

"So?"

"Why'd you come up to me, dude?"

"Oh, it's... I wanted to ask you about Ivy."

"Why, what does she got?"

"Don't you already know?"

"No." Mark shut his locker and slung his bag over a shoulder. He spoke carelessly, without a hint of the aggression Cain expected from male pattern adolescence. Mark shrugged and spoke kindly as if he was letting someone down easy. "Honestly, all my guys are at other schools. I avoid shopping where I work, if you know what I mean."

"I do not."

"I don't like to buy at Seville. I don't want to waste anyone's time. You or Ivy. Sorry."

"It's...okay..."

Cain stood stunned in the middle of the hallway as the homeroom bell rang, sending the hallway into chaos. His phone buzzed in his pocket. It was MaKayla, asking how it went with Mark.

MaKayla

Things were going pretty well. Instead of hiding or ignoring the compulsion to hold the shears, she strapped them to her forearm underneath a long sleeve shirt and an oversized sweater. Not only could she see the interconnectedness of her high school's relationships, but as she focused on the strings, she got better and better at reading the emotions they represented. And those emotions were a welcome distraction from thinking about her mom and how MaKayla may have doomed her parents' marriage.

In Spanish 2, an array of yellows criss-crossed across the rows of thirty desks. From her teacher came four lines, all loving and proud. From most of the students, a line headed toward the exterior wall of the room. MaKayla sensed fear, annoyance, and agitation from most of the faded, tattered lines leading out of the building towards town. Probably family. In another thread, MaKayla discovered a safe, warm friendship between the girls on the soccer team.

"Senorita Colfax? MaKayla Colfax?" her Spanish teacher's deep timber snapped her attention back. "¿Qué acabo de decir?"

"I'm sorry, I zoned out, sir."

"En español, por favor."

"Lamento?"

"Si."

But as her teacher went back to his lesson, MaKayla passed the rest of class in the warmth of the girls' soccer team bond.

She and Cain texted between classes, but she knew he was holding back. Something had obviously happened when he spoke with Mark. It was bothering him, and he wasn't going to text about it. He was such a weirdo, he probably didn't like texting at all.

MaKayla spent the next three periods all in the art studio. She was planning on filming her collage creation to use for another class and maybe early college admission, so she could spend extra time in the laid-back atmosphere of the school's open-air art studio: a big, converted garage at the corner of campus.

She searched through materials, though nothing seemed to be what she was looking for. MaKayla turned down her art teacher's help but noticed something fun on the eccentric woman's tool belt.

The woman had an old leather belt covered in pockets, loops, and compartments filled with paint brushes, scrapers, knives, box cutters, and scissors.

"Is that...a holster for shears?"

"Oh, this? No, I believe it was a part of a belt I made for a friend's Ren faire costume. It hid pepper spray originally, I think."

"How hard was it to make?"

"Took less than an hour. Want to reverse-engineer it?" The teacher removed her work belt and detached the small leather holster. "We definitely have enough leather scraps to cobble one together."

It was a simple concept. A cylinder of hardened leather with a buttoned flap looped over the top. The flap would go down between the two handle grips, and the cylinder keeps the mouth of the scissors closed.

She used the leather-making tools, which took extra muscle and weren't so easy on the hands. But it was a good outlet for her energy. A half hour later, she had the small leather attachment hanging on her own belt. The shears fit perfectly. For a moment, she was a cowboy, quick-drawing her weapon. She even looked pretty cool in the floor-length mirror on the back wall of the studio. With a snap motion, she pulled her scissors out and pointed them at her reflection before twirling them on her finger and then sliding them back into their holster like a quick-drawing cowboy.

"What are you doing? You look ridiculous," Cain admonished her in a whisper, from outside the open garage door.

"I need a better way to carry them," MaKayla said, drawing the shears quickly again.

"Well, you can't have those out where everyone can see."

"Why not?"

"People aren't going to let you walk around in public with a pair of scissors."

He had a point.

"Oh. So what happened with Mark?"

"I had an eye-opening experience with today's youth."

"How on Earth does a seventeen-year-old wind up talking like you?"

"My family... We are eternal—"

"Okay, I apologize for asking. Don't punish me with melodrama. What did Mark say?"

"He tried to purchase drugs from me. Actually, he politely declined to purchase drugs from me. He was very courteous about the entire affair."

"And did you mention Ivy?" MaKayla asked.

"Yes, and he declined to purchase from her as well."

"What?" She could have smacked him if her hand wasn't full of stabby scissors. "Why did he think you were selling drugs? What did you say?"

"I simply greeted him before his assumptions took over."

"And he thought you were selling him drugs?"

"He was confident. And high."

So that was the source of MaKayla's thirst. She felt what Mark felt through the loveline.

"Mark is doing drugs? That doesn't sound like him." This was bad. Mark and Ora were both falling apart. "Besides declining to buy drugs from her, what was his reaction when you mentioned Ivy?"

"That was the only reaction."

"What was his body language saying?"

"'I'm high on drugs.'"

"Was he surprised when you brought her up? Like he was caught?"

"Nope."

"I don't get it. You have to try again."

"No."

"Just try something else."

"No."

"Then just follow him."

Cain let out an annoyed sigh. "I have to work tomorrow."

"Then track him down as a shadow monster."

"What if I say no?"

"Then let me cut their loveline!"

"All you have to do is sever an unassigned connection first."

"I can't find one."

"What about the coach's victims? Everything that man did filled you with disgust; ruined your night pretty fast."

"What he did...that's for a court of law, not for me, to decide."

"Well, the courts decided not to do anything. And his victims are still feeling the way they do. The courts have had their chance, and that chance is gone. So now, the victims are stuck with their feelings, with their connections to that damned tombstone unless you do something."

Sometimes there aren't words that are sad enough or angry enough. Quietly, MaKayla asked, "Will you find out about Mark if I cut one of those ties?"

"Will you tell me the truth?"

She nodded.

"You cut one of those ties, text me, and we can immediately go to sever the bond between Mark and Ora."

Just the idea of slicing the bond sent sensations up her arm. Envisioning the satisfying snip of the shears slicing through thread had MaKayla's fingers flexing. Before she knew it, her hand was on the shear handles.

"You've got to get rid of that holster."

"Well, I can't go around with only one hand free for all of eternity."

"Then find a way to hide it."

She looked in the mirror, twisting her hips to see. The shears on the outside of her clothing were a problem. The metal longed to touch her skin, as her skin longed back. "Maybe I'll attach it to a garter."

Cain gulped.

Cain

He had no idea there were this many baseball games on any given night. But Cain had already followed Mark to three different fields with very active games with invested crowds. Only Mark didn't seem to care about the games.

At the periphery of official events—events like organized sports put together by towns, municipalities, and schools—always lurked the bad kids. They hid under bleachers, out past the home run fences, or behind the concession stands. They smoked cigarettes, hooked up, and more. Cain knew these places intimately, although he'd never frequent them on his own time. There was a special breed of juvenile delinquent who'd go out on a school night just to attend an organized event without paying any attention.

If he'd switched to a human form, Cain would have had plenty of people to hang out with. As someone who ditched regularly, he knew all the delinquents: smokers, druggies, and publicly promiscuous. He also knew that there was usually very little about these kids that was delinquent besides parents they were all too happy to be away from.

Cain stayed in the shadows, hiding from the too-bright game lights, lurking in a darkness of his own. Cain's shadow form could be invisible to the human eye, but the fear that followed affected everyone. The pot smokers got paranoid and scattered. Handsy couples fell out of the mood. But Mark continued on the mission he was on. Cain's presence only seemed to annoy Mark, not scare him.

"You seen Spider?" he asked the group milling around the trees out of ear's reach from the baseball stands. The only answer was shrugs.

He asked the same kids beneath the bleachers. Nothing.

The nearest source of lights past the ball fields was a convenience store. Mark approached a couple of smokers Cain didn't recognize.

"Spider? Whatchu' want with Spider?" The bigger guy mumbled from under the low brim of a hat.

"I just want to see what he's got."

The meaner looking guy stood quickly and approached. "Wanna see what we got?" he hissed.

"You want pills or something else?" the big guy asked, taking a step into the parking lot, in the opposite direction of the mean guy.

They were flanking him, whether Mark saw it or not. He just kept talking to the bigger one. With a step closer, Mark asked, "What kind of pills you got?"

"You got cash?" The mean one took a step further into the empty parking lot, blocking the easy way out.

"Yeah, you know what I got..." Mark reached in his pockets, fumbling, as he scooted in further to the big guy, who was ready to pounce.

It was all coming together so clearly for Cain; an unassuming mouse, merely wandering into a trap. Poor Mark must've been quite inebriated. And Cain was just supposed to watch? This was in no way fair. The least Cain could do was make this a fair fight.

From beneath the dumpster, Cain's shadow pooled and moved across the parking lot, running up the mean guy's legs to engulf him and stun him in the throes of awe.

Just then, Mark made his move. He turned and bolted from the bigger guy into a sprint straight for the mean guy. And not for the easy way out; Mark was charging the mean guy...who was paralyzed in fear.

Mark tackled him, and the two tumbled across the pavement as Cain's shadow receded. Now Cain didn't know how to help, or if he should. But then the bigger guy rushed up holding a knife that Mark couldn't see; they were going to have Mark surrounded all over again. Only closer, armed, and pissed off.

Cain stepped out from the shadows and announced, "Hey, get the hell away from him, you two!" before turning to call out behind him, "Hey guys, over here! It's Mark!"

It was a bluff, but Cain didn't really know what else to do that didn't involve doing harm to all three humans. So he bluffed. And he leaned into it, sprinting right at them.

Whatever Cain was thinking, running in his mortal human form straight for a mugger with a knife, it worked. The two guys ran off.

Standing in his ready-to-fight position, out of breath, Mark's eyes were frozen wide. "You saved me, drug dealer!"

"Do not call me that."

Mark turned to look after the running assailants, then back to Cain, eyes still wide. "You saved me?"

"I guess."

"You. saved." Mark burst out laughing and roared, "Me!"

"Unnecessarily loud," Cain said, somewhat to himself over Mark's laughter.

"I'm still not buying off you, but thanks."

"I am not a drug dealer."

"Then why are you here?"

"The hospital's nearby. I know someone there," Cain fumbled awkwardly with the explanation, trying to make it sound like a normal thing that no one would ask more questions about. "He's dying."

"Oh, yeah?" Mark seemed interested. He pulled out a cigarette and lit it, asking, "Does he know he's dying?"

"Yeah."

"How's he taking it?"

This was having the opposite effect that Cain had intended. He sighed, "He's...fighting it."

"Good for him," Mark said, unscrewing a flask he suddenly had. He offered it to Cain.

Cain politely declined, but Mark insisted.

Why not? If Cain got inebriated, simply phasing through dimensions would shake any buzz he could get. So, he accepted the small plastic bottle.

Cain had drank before. Plenty of wine at home and a beer at a couple parties. But not liquor. He knocked back a hefty gulp.

"Do you believe in fate, Cain?"

Cain's eyes shot wide as he gasped the tail-end of his drink of vodka. Then a small burp. Then coughing. Endless coughing. He was red-faced and hoarse from coughing and he wound up sitting down on now-wet concrete beside Mark, who was kindly patting his newfound friend on the back.

"You're a funny guy, Morrigan. Destiny's got me—I have visions of it. Ora and I together. Fighting against the world, and we only have each other. For years and years until I die. No escaping that."

Cain cleared his throat several times, then managed, "And you believe that your dreams or what have you are your fate?"

"I believe what I see," Mark said, then took a sip from the flask.

"Well, fine. If it's destiny, it'll happen. You shouldn't feel obligated to try and follow the path. Any path should lead you there."

"You know what, Morrigan?" Mark asked.

"What?"

"You have no idea what you're talking about." Mark struggled to his feet, cigarette dangling from his lip as he put the flask away. "But thanks for saving my life." Mark took steps away from the convenience store. "By the way...you should watch it with Ivy Skelton."

"Why? What do you know about her? Did y'all like, mess around?"

Mark chuckled, took one long drag, then stomped the life out of the cigarette. "No. I just saw her go mental on my girlfriend for not taking her Bible study or something seriously. Like, turned stalker."

Cain was about to pry to get more info about Mark and Ivy, but just wanted the conversation to end. Except a curiosity for MaKayla's sake. Maybe Cain was a bit worried for her and what ignoring a heartstring was doing to her. So he asked Mark, "Are you and Ora cool?"

"She's my destiny, Morrigan. You wouldn't get it." And then Mark walked off.

Cain couldn't decide if the poor jock was limping or staggering away, but he considered shadowing him to make sure he got home safe.

"You should listen to him, you know. I get good kids into bad trouble," a hoarse voice teased from behind him.

People didn't usually sneak up on Cain. He played it cool, answering without turning, "I'm not that good of a kid."

Ivy teased, "I'm flattered you're asking around about me. Does this mean you're not still pissed I treated you like garbage?"

"Maybe I've been treated worse."

"I bet you have." She stood next to him, though they didn't face each other, just continued looking out into the gently falling snow. "I was outside the hospital, and I thought I heard someone fighting."

"Yeah, it looked like some guys were going to jump him."

"And you swooped in to save the day? Wow."

"I wouldn't say that."

She let out a deep sigh, traces of steam billowing out into the dark. "You're really a nice guy, aren't you, Cain Morrigan?"

"I wouldn't say that either."

"I would." Then she dropped away, no longer at his side. She said, "Listen to Mark and stay away from me. For your own good."

"Aren't you the one who just walked up to me?"

"I wanted to see. And now I'm the one walking away."

And she left Cain there in the drifting snow alone with conflicting thoughts drifting through his mind like the snowflakes that surrounded him.

Chapter 9

MaKayla

She gave up—MaKayla agreed to snip a heartstring from the cemetery. Hopefully to save someone from some toxic connection to their abuser.

Just thinking about it absolutely broke her heart. MaKayla had never been abused like that; intimately, repeatedly. But she knew plenty of kids who had. There wasn't a year went by there wasn't a local story from Lockport or a town nearby of some doctor, teacher, priest, or coach who didn't misuse their position to steal some poor kid's childhood. It was always someone close like that, or even an uncle. Never the trans or gay bogeyman that she'd never heard of. Those so-called villains had plenty of laws. Meanwhile, people like that coach took so many connections with him. He must have operated like that for years, maybe decades.

Maybe MaKayla was justifying the decision she was about to make. Maybe she was trying to warm herself from the inside with her rage.

The snow was just beginning to stick, dotting the late April night in a layer of reflective white, the falling flakes making it way too bright for this late. Breath curled up around MaKayla's head in uneven spurts as she shifted weight back and forth so fast that she was almost jogging in place.

"Thanks for texting me back," Cain said, although it scared the b'Jesus out of MaKayla, so she jumped and squeaked and only heard, 'Thanks.'

"You can't just pop up behind me and talk like that, man."

"I'm sorry. Shall I step on a twig next time?"

"Next time, walk up to me like a human. If you just...vampired here, does that mean I'm driving us to the graveyard?"

"Cemetery," he corrected her. "And no, it'd be much faster if you'd just come with me."

"Does that entail, like, opening a portal to Hell or something similarly awful?"

"I doubt you could even travel by shadow," he said in a derisive way, although MaKayla definitely didn't take it bad.

"Shall it be steam locomotive, then, m'Lord?" she asked in a terrible, implacable accent.

"We'll fly. Just... give me a moment to change forms." And he headed around the building.

"Okay..." MaKayla followed, giving him plenty of space.

By the time she rounded the corner, Cain was in a grassy patch behind the dumpsters. "Kindly stay back. And maybe avert your eyes. I haven't ever done this in front of a human."

"Sure." MaKayla turned, watching snow slowly overtake the pair of footprints they'd left. With them side by side, she observed that his feet weren't that big; their feet were almost the same size. This made her chuckle a bit. Maybe that was why Cain tried so hard to put up a tough front. She tried not to laugh out loud at the clumsy sound of Cain fumbling his clothes off behind her. To whatever this embarrassing other form was.

His shadow form had been truly terrifying; that was the most scared she'd ever been, but now that it was over, it was easy to think of it as thrilling. So much so, that she almost wanted to see it again. Almost.

She wasn't sure what to expect, maybe something diminutive like a bat. Wait. Was this guy some kind of vampire? The idea started making sense to MaKayla when she felt a surge. A charging, like a sudden movement of static electricity rushing from the soles of her feet to the top of her head, and then a deafening crack, like the snapping of a tree branch.

She couldn't help but turn, to see what destruction was behind her, dangerously close to Cain. The dumpster sat still in the bluish snow light. No trace of Cain.

Instinctively, she ran over to look for him, searching for any sign of a collision or downed trees. Nothing. But there, behind the dumpster and nearly the side of it, a black rock. Cain's clothes were in a neat pile by the dumpster, but where was he?

The black rock, or boulder rather, didn't catch any of the giant drifting snowflakes. The color was a deep, velvety black that reflected none of the evening light, seemingly sucking the light from the air around it.

The surface was so dark, MaKayla couldn't make out the texture of the rock. Or maybe it was some type of pod or egg housing Cain? As she reached out to it, the slow downward drift of the snow shifted, all flakes abruptly turning south. The wind pushed MaKayla's chestnut hair into her face. Brushing it away, the surface of the rock appeared to be blowing in the wind in some way.

MaKayla leaned in closer to see tiny movement all over...

Then the rock moved. Suddenly, like the Earth itself was

quaking and shattering, the rock bloomed open. Its black surface broke into plates of fine fur. No, not fur–feathers. The blackest of feathers on enormous wings stretching, open- ing, reaching out and up into the snowy, windy night. And underneath them, a figure, shaped like a human male, stood inhumanly tall, his face overcast with shadow but his skin ghostly pale. If he were still, he'd be an alabaster statue left in the dark.

His enormous wings spread wide, unbelievably wide, a horizon of blackness before her, broken up by his long pale body. Even in the bright snowy night, a thin sheet of white now topping cars and the dumpster and the branches of trees, he stayed unnaturally shaded with wings behind him, exposing the monolith of his body and long, cascading hair down to his knees. Growing not just from his head, but down his neck, onto his shoulders, and she assumed down his back. His hair was blue-black; a stark shining contrast to his blacker-than-black wings.

Exaggerated, elongated, it was Cain, but more Cain than she'd ever seen. Musculature carved deep and defined still left him lean and long, towering.

His gauntness and sharp chin were now a crescent-mooned face. And his eyes... oh, those eyes.

MaKayla was staring. Hard. And honestly, she didn't care. His exaggerated features, lightless body, and near-nudity made MaKayla weak—in several parts of her own body and maybe her mind. She knew she shouldn't be gawking at him, especially not back and forth from his eyes to the hair blocking his nudity, but this way-too-serious boy at her school, with all of this impossible knowledge and a paranormal dark side, stood like a statue of a god.

Determined to speak like a normal person, MaKayla had to swallow deeply twice and clear her throat. "So..." She cleared her throat again. "How many forms do you have?"

"More than I know."

Something about his answer took her breath away. She too often forgot what a mysterious creature Cain Morrigan was. "What are you?" she asked, afraid of the truth.

He opened his arms wide. "Your best chance at fulfilling your potential."

For a moment, it felt funny, like an important decision to make: whether or not to trust this person-slash-shadow monster-slash-deity, who came into her life only days ago. But this was also a perversion of countless conversations she'd had with her mom, who'd always assured MaKayla that she was the only one who'd ever understand their power, their Fatehood. Mom was the one who'd always be there. *Mom* was always supposed to be MaKayla's best, if not only, chance at fulfilling her potential.

Nope. It was the emo kid a grade ahead of her who was secretly eight feet tall with midnight black wings. Whether she shrugged or even whispered 'F—— it,' to herself or not, she conceded to join him, trust him, and stand on his overgrown bare feet while he hugged her.

His wings didn't flap, and he didn't leap to get them in the air. They simply ascended together as if pulled to the heavens by sheer will. The ground flew away below, leaving behind the settling snow, the dumpster, and MaKayla's stomach. Wind blew across her face, stinging cold telling her how fast they flew. She wanted to spin, to barrel roll, to loopty-loop, to scream into the night, declaring the world was theirs simply for their ability to rise above it, to see the dirty-dotted white landscape at such a height that mankind and even their work was practically unnoticeable.

How could Cain ever come down? What would possess a person to give up this majesty, this perspective of unrelenting beauty? She caught herself gaping at him again: his smooth, pale-yet-darkened skin, his ribbons of hair flapping and undulating, his luminous eyes. How could he ever choose another form besides this? But more importantly, how could MaKayla ever look at him the same way again? How could she be expected to talk to him like another student after seeing what he was, his potential form? Was it lust or love that stirred within her as her eyes traced the shape of each fine bulging muscle?

Even after they landed, could she ever see her world the same again? Could she ever come down from this high?

Cain

Flight while holding another person was a slower process, and rather annoying. This was going horribly. Between the extra weight of a passenger and the headwind, there was no way it was faster to fly to the cemetery than drive. And time was running out for Cain and his assignment.

For once, though, MaKayla didn't have a sarcastic comment to belittle Cain or undermine his authority as an expert. She seemed so distracted by his appearance in his angelic form that she didn't notice the extra travel time.

If he had any pigment in his skin, he'd be burning in embarrassment the way MaKayla stared at him. He'd never shared this side of himself with anyone before, and knew, or at least had some idea how strange he appeared. Elfin features and sallow complexion...not to mention that this form wouldn't hold clothes. It was all so embarrassing. He looked absurd and felt utterly exposed.

But he couldn't travel with her in his Reaper form, not without separating her soul from this mortal coil. And he couldn't fly in any other form unless he became some animal. For some reason, he couldn't stand the idea of being driven around by the girl who he was supposed to be mentoring. She was unruly enough as a mentee; something about politely sitting in her passenger seat sounded unbearable.

Any minute, MaKayla would make some comment about how farcical this form looked. But it never came, and they successfully floated over the sleepy town of Lockport, New York, nestled under a fluffy layer of white. Finally, they landed in the middle of the short hill of untouched snow, in front of the headstrong with dozens of heartstrings arcing out like rays of sunlight.

They pretty much were just light to Cain. A Reaper couldn't touch the threads, at least not like a Fate. He simply walked straight through them, backing away from MaKayla, giving her the space to do what she agreed to. She kept eye contact, a pleading look. Cain wasn't sure if she just didn't want to do this or was actually unable to cut unassigned threads. But he was determined to get it over with and find out.

He kept backing away, giving her space, even if he felt a little compelled to run to her, to find out what those big, expressive dark eyes wanted from him. Something in him wanted to stop torturing her, stop forcing her to ignore the compulsion of the shears. This was hurting her, maybe even physically, and he wanted it to stop.

What was he even doing, lying to her like this? By now, she knew as much about being a Fate as he did. He had nothing to teach her. And here she was, trusting him, listening to him (in her own way), not openly mocking his other forms, which he'd always expected from humans. But she wasn't human, was she? She was a Fate, a 'capital F' Fate. An immortal presiding over life, like him.

This was all wrong, the way he was using her; although he couldn't tell her the truth. But he could do the next best thing; teach her as much as he could, tell her as much truth as he could, without endangering his own chances of becoming a full Reaper.

Thankfully, she tore away those warm, dark brown eyes from his and quickly set to work, scrutinizing the threads coming off the headstone. Her eyes focused on one line as she reached out to touch it with her fingertips. Her face grew heavy with whatever feelings she was receiving from the thread. From the scrunching of her eyebrows and the light dancing in the corner of her eyes, she must have been sensing so much sadness. She moved on to the next loveline and gasped softly before immediately releasing it.

Going from thread to thread, MaKayla was getting more and more upset, tears welling in her eyes and then dashing down her cheeks. Her breath grew increasingly frustrated, full of gasps and sighs. She started muttering to herself, growing increasingly frustrated with each thread. Cain could barely catch her words.

"...no, not you...

"...she helps victims now, recounts her abuse...

"...No, Coach...

"...used it as motivation to save a life...

"...this guy actually loved this monster...

"...enabled him for years...

"...stop it, Coach...

"...dear God, what was wrong with this man?!"

She fell to her knees in front of the headstone, and again Cain had to prevent himself from rushing to her. Sure, he'd understood that she was different, that she was superhuman, but he'd still thought of her as below a Reaper. She wasn't as powerful of a being, but he couldn't feel connections like she could. He couldn't understand the delicate relationships between these fragile beings like she could. Did that make her somehow stronger than him? Stronger than other Reapers?

She got to her feet, unbuttoning her big outer coat, withdrawing the shears from somewhere. Trapping one thread between her index finger and thumb, she leaned in, looking down the line reaching out from the cemetery to the horizon, laying an ear so gently along the taut wire.

With a slick sound, the shears opened. The angled mouth of the blades pushed into the heartstring.

She closed her eyes. He found himself leaning forward in anticipation. She squeezed the scissors shut.

Snip.

Ivy

"You should lie back," Ivy said gently, removing the old book from her grandfather's lap.

"And you should prepare the vessel."

The vessel. Always the vessel.

Ivy knew her expression soured, that she was most likely

glaring, but Grandpa was focused out the window.

"Where are you, my adjutant angel?" he said to no one in particular. Maybe his reflection. He barely spoke to Ivy anymore.

They were both getting impatient. There hadn't been another sighting of the dark figure, and Ivy wasn't ready to tell him everything she knew.

Cain Morrigan was the lickspittle Reaper, and Ivy had done everything short of warning him what was to come.

The old man was dying soon, that was certain, but there was no certainty his plan would unfold. Their plan. She wasn't ready to watch one of her classmates die for him. Not even for their decade of work. But she also didn't know if she could stand up to Grandpa if the moment came.

She was getting soft. Ivy from a month ago would have told Grandpa the truth about Cain Morrigan. Ivy from a month ago was done with people, was ready for whatever was next, whatever Grandpa had promised, their impossible plans for immortality. She had smiled when the runes burned into her skin for the first time. She recited more incantations as the burning got worse. And she had eaten up every word Grandpa had to offer, even the insults and sexist proclamations.

Heartbreak had set her free from humanity, so why did she still have this soft spot for that idiot Cain Morrigan? Sure, he was cute and incredibly oblivious. And if it was really true, what he was, then...he was something else.

But something about his dopey face stopped her from completely selling him out before it was necessary. It was stupid of her, and she knew it. She should have said something to Grandpa right then. But she just let the milky-eyed old man stare out the window into the snowy night.

For now, she hoped Cain Morrigan had heeded her warning and would leave Grandpa's soul for another Grim Reaper to take.

MaKayla

What on Earth was Cain Morrigan? She kept coming back to that question as she walked into his arms onto his feet again. Again, she stared at his exaggerated muscles, his magnified eyes. Again, she felt repulsed by, and attracted to this guy who was way more than a guy. No matter how godlike he looked then, she'd always resent him for making her cut that thread.

It was not a satisfying sound or sensation. There was no joy at seeing the ends of threads rebounding, recoiling back into nothingness.

"Let's go to Ora's?" she asked, devoid of emotion.

"Are you alright?"

She slid her arms around his waist, resting her head against his chest. "Can we go to Ora's now, please?"

"Hey…" He trailed off, inviting her to look up at him.

But she couldn't. He probably couldn't help the amount of pity in his big, cartoonishly blue eyes. She didn't want his sympathy; she only wanted the nightmarish compulsion to end, to silence the nagging voice constantly telling her to sever Ora's relationship…

But even with his face full of unwanted sympathy, he was gorgeous. Beautiful like a supermodel — surreal, supernatural, and alien. Features so flawless, they didn't belong on this planet. He didn't belong here among mortals. Because he wasn't mortal. He was something else.

She was something else, too, but not something beautiful. She was not shifting skins dancing across the planes of existence like Cain. She was not such an adventure as him. She was the end to the adventure, the punctuation to prove things finite, the abrupt stop, leaving lifetimes of things unfinished.

What would this life be, to give in to these powers, these responsibilities? Was she destined to become her mother in the most sinister ways?

"How is the severing...affecting you?"

Her eyes were closed, listening to his breathing, uneasy from his lack of a heartbeat in this form. Opening them meant seeing the heights, seeing all of Lockport, its people so small. Small people beneath the two of them. She and this deity flying her across the sky. She wasn't ready to open her eyes and look down on all of humanity. Not yet.

"All that matters is severing Ora and Mark. I'll be fine after that."

"You're not fine."

"It's not the severing. It's not being able to help any of those people. For whatever this is, this gift or curse, for all of the power and duty or whatever, I couldn't help a single person at the other end of those heartstrings."

"You helped one."

Her answer stewed in her stomach and bubbled up, leaving a sour taste souring her own expression. "No. No, I didn't. I couldn't help any of Coach's victims. It's not up to me to fix someone else. I can't just cut away their trauma, trim off a memory, and pat myself on the back for a job well done. It's their trauma. It's theirs. Hopefully to work through in a healthy way, but. It's. Theirs. I don't care what I am; I'm not making those decisions for others. I found a guy who stood up for

Coach." Remembering curled up her lips in a disgusted smile. "A guy who wouldn't let anyone talk bad about Coach in bars or at parties or at the office. The guy who signed the petition to name the gym after Coach. The guy who was getting sick and tired of people he thought were lying to get attention and attack the character of a man as good as Coach." Her throat dried out, and her breath died with the words.

They flew quietly, the whoosh of wind and the angle of his feet her only clues that they were in the air.

"But for the sake of training, no. No negative effects from 'severing an unassigned heartstring,'" she said the last word with an acidic sting. She'd never think of these connections the same ever again. It wasn't the love that manifested as the threads; it was simply the strength of the emotion.

Of course, she still had a million questions about being a Fate, about the shears and the strings, but she always would. There was only so much that Cain would be able to teach her. He wasn't a Fate himself, whatever he was. And Mom never let herself become a Fate. Besides, there was no knowing how much Mom would even be in her life anymore.

So MaKayla had a lifetime of piecing this together as she went. And maybe it wasn't so bad having Cain around while she was just getting her feet. She needed someone to lean on, and even if he acted like he knew more than he probably did, something told her she could trust him.

She opened her eyes. Far below, the town passed beneath them, iced in accumulating snow. But cutting through the night, filling the white terrain with angles and shapes and overlap and weave, were heartstrings. Connections of love and hate running throughout her hometown. People being held together in a way not many could see, not like her.

Beautiful.

It was probably the first time since getting her shears that she actually enjoyed being a Fate.

She recognized the Mark and Ora heartstring from a literal mile away.

"We can land here."

"Aurora's all the way on the other side of the canal—"

"The loveline is down there, though. I see it. I feel it."

They landed in the bluish-white night, thick flakes slowly cascading down. The thread sang out to her like a siren, beckoning her. Cutting across the canal-side park, the graying string sat taut at MaKayla's eye level. Her steps crunched across the field, leaving a trail of tracks melted in the ground.

Cain stayed back.

MaKayla moved automatically. Instinct took over her body. Or maybe it was the shears operating her body like a car. Footsteps continued crunching. Tearing off a glove, she unsheathed the shears. All in one liquid, unstopping motion, she opened the shears, continued walking, and brought her intersecting blades up to the thread.

Snip.

Her feet kept moving, but she wasn't walking. She was relaxing. Every part of her body relaxed, muscles letting go of days' worth of tension as her body staggered along to keep up with her feet. First dropping her outstretched scissor arm, then her shoulders and back, letting go of all of the anxiety from the thread's non-stop chatter, MaKayla stumbled.

In her mind, silence. Her thoughts, the scissors, and all potential assigned heartstrings muted at once. And within a quiet mind, MaKayla drifted off to sleep.

The bright blue snowy world faded to black.

Cain

On the flight home, MaKayla stayed in a deep sleep in Cain's arms. The wind blew strands of hair across her face no matter how many times he brushed it back. She seemed peaceful. Her face slack, her body boneless. Still darkened red beneath each eye and pallor to her lips, she was obviously exhausted. But Cain knew it was the emotional weight of severing the loveline, and not the act of severance, that drained her. This fatigue of her human body was from procrastination. It was his fault.

Cain and other Reapers evidently weren't physically tied to assignments like Fates, or at least not like this Fate. And here he'd been, pretending to know so much, pretending to help her, to guide her safely in understanding and mastering her powers. And he didn't understand any of it.

Disgust in himself slowly filled him like bile. How could he have been so selfish? With such a physical toll on her, it was very possible that using her like this could have seriously hurt her. Or worse.

At that moment, cradling her vulnerable, slumbering body, he would do anything to protect her, to keep her safe.

He had to keep her safe from himself. He had to end this selfish use of her. He knew what he had to do then. Not just drop her off and schedule the severing of the Skelton heartstring for tomorrow. Sailing across the snow clouds over upstate New York, Cain dropped his plan. He would find another way of culling the Skelton soul, even if he only had one day. He saw it in the distance, at the tall brick hospital building, a bright golden rope connecting a top corner window to a house across the canal.

The old man's words taunted Cain. He could think of nothing

else the rest of their night flight. *"Death cannot touch me, Lickspittle. Not so long as I have this."*

He only had two days. He had to think of something, but he would not allow himself to use MaKayla any further.

Landing softly on the roof outside of MaKayla's bedroom window, he sat her up to unlock and open the window, then remove the screen. She stirred to a drowsy alertness by the time he picked her up.

As he lifted her, she clasped her clammy hands behind his neck. She leaned in, so close, he could feel her hot breath. In his ear, she whispered softly, "My butt's wet."

Getting her into bed felt similar to dealing with a drunk. Simply with the difficulty of removing her coat and wet boots, Cain quickly gave up on the idea of changing her into sleepwear or even gently tucking her in. She basically fought him just getting her winter hat off and laying down on her bed.

Her phone pinged.

"Whosit?" She wasn't even opening her eyes.

He tried ignoring her, covering her with a blanket.

"Whosit?" she asked louder through closed eyes.

He hushed her and checked. "Mom."

"Whashesay?"

"I don't know. Your phone's locked."

"Oh-six-two-oh-sixty-nine."

"Your birth month and sixty-nine? You're ridiculous."

"You're ridiculous." She turned over, gripping and nuzzling a pillow. "Whashesay?"

"'We need to talk. I'll see you tomorrow. I know you're off work.'"

MaKayla was snoring by the time Cain finished reading the message.

Chapter 10

MaKayla

"I'm not your enemy, MaKayla. I'm the only person on Earth who actually understands what you're going through."

MaKayla stayed hidden behind her sunglasses, staring down her mother while lunching in the windowed room of the nicest Italian restaurant in Lockport. Mom loved this place—not any of the food, but the status of it all, the pomp and circumstance of dressing for a fine meal.

Mom was picking around her plate, talking and not eating. MaKayla was ravenous. She'd woken up hungry and had taken out a pretty serious breakfast before staring at her art project for nearly an hour without adding anything to it. Now she was scarfing down an antipasto salad with bread, doing her best to listen.

"I screwed up with your father. Big time. He doesn't really... know my background. Nobody really does. No one left alive."

Mom had always been hyperbolic in big talks with her kids, but this was a stretch even for her. MaKayla couldn't fault her, though. She woke up so relaxed and refreshed, she couldn't even get angry. This was a tough time in her parents' marriage, and if her mom needed to unburden herself, MaKayla could put up with it. She was hungry enough, and the salad was amazing. Once she was full, maybe she'd be able to get angry again.

The truth was, she wasn't feeling much of anything at all since snipping apart Mark and Ora. It had emptied her anxiety cup completely, and she actually had the emotional bandwidth right now to deal with her mom.

MaKayla had been so angry. At her mom, but then at herself for allowing Cain to reveal the truth about the gun in the house. But that guilt wasn't MaKayla's to carry. And she was no longer in the dark about who she was, what she was, and the power she wielded. By the time she'd agreed to brunch and sat down to eat, MaKayla only wanted to ease some of Mom's pain. So MaKayla listened.

"But," her mom said in a hoarse, even tone, "even without telling him about the scissors and the madness that came with them, I should have told him I was keeping a gun in the house. And I should have been honest with you and your brother, too." Mom's voice broke. She looked like she hadn't been sleeping or maybe just crying a lot. "So before I say anything else, I must say that I am truly, truly sorry, buttercup." She held and squeezed MaKayla's hand across the table, then took a sip of wine. Clearing her throat and furrowing her eyebrow, Mom changed her tone completely, whispering accusingly, "You used the scissors last night."

MaKayla suddenly felt something. Her stomach clenched enough to make her wonder whether it would hold down the salad.

"Twice, I believe. That is dangerous, young lady. I wasn't

holding mine, and I am no longer practicing any form of diablerie, but I can sense that you did. I guarantee you others did as well. There is a big world out there, a big, dark, scary world that most people are lucky enough to live their entire lives without knowing about. Your father and your brother, hopefully. And you have a chance to get out now, MaKayla. You can get out with the sliver that you know. Because there are things out there more powerful than us. I've seen things and done things, bad things to some—"

"How is everything?" the perky waitress popped her head in.

The silence was so awkward, MaKayla couldn't help but snicker.

"Just the check." Mom smiled until the waitress was out of earshot, then said, "MaKayla, this is serious. Bigger than you and me. Bigger than life or death. Now you will be approached by strangers in the near future. Powerful people who will sense who and what you are and come looking."

"To kill me?"

"To use you, without a doubt. But kill you? Maybe, yes."

"Is that what you used to do? Kill people"

Mom's silence answered MaKayla's question and tilted her world a bit. The mother she thought she knew never existed. 'Mom' was an act, just a persona she put on after living a much more dangerous life.

"Can we talk more about...about what you know? Can I trust you to teach me?"

"Oh, buttercup." Again, Mom reached across the restaurant table and squeezed MaKayla's hand, only this time, Mom was a completely different woman than she had been five minutes ago. And this was now a completely different relationship.

"I'll be around some. Someone from my days of diablerie

has called in a favor. Give me a few days, then we can talk more at length. But MaKayla, you have to be willing to listen to me. This isn't like flunking math or losing a nice coat I bought you."

"I don't know what diablerie means."

"It's...complicated; the imbalance of humanity's place in nature, enlightenment, sorcery."

"Sorcery? I thought you locked your shears away."

"There's much scarier and more powerful things out there than scissors, MaKayla. You keep playing with yours, I guarantee you'll find out. What I can't guarantee is that I'll be there to protect you when that happens."

"Okay, Mom."

"I hope you're taking this seriously, MaKayla."

"I am."

And with those two words, the role of 'Mom' was assumed once more, and MaKayla played her part of daughter, casually ignoring the fact that her mom was most likely a killer. But she was also still Mom. Still manipulative, still narcissistic. Sure, she'd teach MaKayla, maybe even save her life, but Mom would have to be in control. And Mom would have to be constantly thanked and fawned over. It was the same relationship as always, even if the stakes had grown supernatural. MaKayla's mom would never change.

As soon as her mom left, MaKayla checked her phone. She'd been messaging with Cain all day, and his responses had been the same since the early morning, every couple of hours.

"Still in the Library."

At first, it was such an exciting idea. She'd texted back, *"The Library?! THE Library?! The Library of Forbidden Knowledge?!"*

"..."

"The Library."

But the idea of a library lost its novelty after he'd been there for eight hours.

"Are we meeting tonight?"

He responded, *"I actually wanted to talk..."*

Oh, that's never a good thing to hear. MaKayla had woken up in such a good mood, she wasn't ready for another overly serious chat. And then she had to stare at the dreaded ellipses. He was replying, she was just doomed to wait. Damn ellipses. What, was he writing a novel?

"I wanted to bring you here."

Her stomach literally fluttered, and she hated her gut for it. He wanted her *there*? At the Library of Forbidden Knowledge? Maybe it was a small difference in phrasing, but nothing about the way Cain had approached mentoring her ever felt like he *wanted* to. He never made it seem like he *wanted* her around or *wanted* to teach her something—it was all compulsory.

And of course, she'd always been interested in the library, especially a Library of Forbidden Knowledge. But he *wanted* her there?

She pictured him saying it to her, looking deep into her eyes without his facade of snobbery about humanity. And she couldn't help but picture him in his godly form, larger than life, towering over her with an unreal physique, gorgeous straight hair, and eyes that swallowed her up. No training, no lovestrings, just him being real with her, telling her he wanted to show her something. That he wanted her. He needed her...

She was biting her lip. Oh no, was she catching feelings for this guy?

No. He'd put her through so many headaches in only a matter of days and did it with a smirk on his face as if he expected her to thank him. He'd been a jerk to her this entire week, and not just the constant condescension but the mental anguish of his forcing her to delay snipping Mark and Ora's loveline.

But the idea that Cain was thinking of her, that he wanted to do something for her... It may not have completely made up for how he had treated her, but she suddenly wanted to see this side of him. She wanted to see Cain in a position of trying to please her. She wanted to see him make it up to her.

But maybe she just wanted to see him.

"Sure, what's the address?"

Cain

This was bad. There were no answers. No alternatives to how Reapers severed lovelines, how occult practitioners were vanquished, or how sick and ready souls could be easily culled. For a library, this place was pretty unhelpful.

So why invite MaKayla? It was just another way to highlight how Cain had absolutely no idea what he was doing. He had until tomorrow night, but couldn't bring himself to go through with the only way he knew to cull his assigned soul.

On another castle-door table, he'd gathered all of the tomes and scrolls he found that mentioned Fates, heartstrings, or even Greek mythological bloodlines. It wasn't much, but at least he could give her all the information he had, to make up for lying to her.

Which brought him back to that nagging feeling; he had to tell her the truth. He had to admit exactly what he was, the details of his latest assignment, and how he'd planned on using her and her bloodline's abilities in order to complete his assignment. How he was actually going to break it to her was still unknown.

So in between cross-referencing Wikipedia pages to some of the actual primary sources, such as cuneiform tablets or Aramaic scrolls, he practiced his confession.

"MaKayla, there's something you should know, something I have to confess. I am a Reaper. That's not the confession—I just owed you that fact, too. The truth is, I lied. I don't know anything about Fates. I wasn't sent to train you. I saw you in the halls, tracing a loveline. Hell, it might have been the first time you'd seen them. Then I got assigned a soul to cull, and something was amiss; the soul is tethered to the physical world. By a loveline. My plan was to pretend to train you in order to see if you could help me. Then use your powers so I could cull the soul. I'm sorry, and I was wrong. But I'm not going to use you like that, I can't. I've got a new plan of attack, because now I've got feelings for you—"

His phone pinged. New text from MaKayla.

Even with the sudden rush of serotonin and numb feeling in his toes at the thought of her, Cain prepared himself for yet another "still at the library" response. It had been five hours, and he hadn't found any more information about the possible Grandpa Skelton loveline or how he could have possibly been able to identify Cain as a Reaper.

So instead, Cain focused on what he *could* do and studied up on shifting to a form he'd never tried, one that would allow him to sneak up on Grandpa Skelton. He delved into the history of the Reapers, a power set long forgotten. Through ages-old writings, he reconnected with an ancient truth about himself.

But now he was getting a text from a girl.

"Just pulled up to your house."

Cain had never shifted into his shadow form faster. He was

barely materialized by the time he opened the front door. He knew he had to beat his mom to answer it, but she was nowhere to be seen.

Cain went outside, just as MaKayla got out of her car to walk up. Weekend MaKayla, all bundled up in the relentless snow, appeared even more charming than in her school or work appearances. She had a short puffy jacket with fur accents, tight black pants, and big fur-lined snow boots. Her hat was also furry and big, giving MaKayla Colfax an entirely different silhouette. In fact, her shape was so different and interesting, Cain caught himself staring as she walked up the thin strip of salted slick gray walkway that broke up the thick white snow.

MaKayla walked with purpose and bounce, her hips giving in to each step, her figure tilting from side to side in a way that stirred something in Cain.

"How'd it go with your Mom?"

"Every time that woman attempts to explain something to me, I always leave more confused and with more questions than I started with. Do you know anything about diablerie?"

"What, like thaumaturgy?"

"I have no idea what that is, either."

"It literally means devilry, but in practice is more akin to... magic?"

"Magic? Well, Mom's warning me against a life of magic, then."

"Yeah, but it can be more complicated than just that. There's dozens of different approaches to defining diablerie to be found, just in the library alone."

"Oh man, I can't wait to see it."

"And you will. You deserve to. MaKayla, there's something you should know, something I have to confess. I—"

"Is there any chance this can wait? I'm having a real hard time giving too much attention to anything when I'm so close to a Library of Forbidden Knowledge. Like...if you show it to me, will the knowledge literally kill me?"

Cain stuttered, "No, not at all."

"Good."

But then he realized he wasn't completely certain of the answer, adding, "As long as you have your scissors."

"Oh..."

"...I think."

"You think? You're not sure whether your library will kill me or not, you just 'think'?"

"Well, you have them, don't you?"

"Of course, I do; that's not the point." She was quiet for a second after having removed all her winter outerwear. Then she softened. "I still want to see it."

"There's time for that later. I'd really like to talk."

"Dude. You're a very interesting guy and even cute, especially when you turn super-sized, but there is a *Library of Forbidden Knowledge*. Right past that door. It may not be that cool to you because it's been in your house your entire life, but to me, it may be the literally coolest thing on Earth. Unless maybe there was a museum of forbidden art, too."

"Oh, the library has halls and halls of art."

"Then shut up and show me."

MaKayla

She couldn't believe she'd called him cute. Embarrassment simmered in her chest the entire walk down the never-ending stone staircase. All she could do the entire trip following Cain's electric lamp down the winding tunnels was replay the embarrassing moment in her head over and over.

The problem was that when she looked at Cain now, she always saw him in his angel form. Godlike form was more accurate, as he'd been inhumanly tall, ripped with tea saucer-sized crystal blue eyes. But now she was noticing his everyday human form, how sharp his cheekbones and chin were, how sleek his jaw. And those eyes. And those crystalline blues were still big enough to trip MaKayla over her own words.

As they descended, MaKayla's eyes trained on Cain's wide and sleek back. Outside of school, he still dressed the same: black on black on black. But at least at home, he had no bulky coat, sweater, or book bag. He was in a tight, long-sleeve black shirt, old and fraying at the seams but hugging his sleek figure, long and lean but still muscled and V-shaped. And as they reached the bottom of the stairs, MaKayla could get a good look at his round butt filling out his black jeans.

"What are you doing?" he asked abruptly, as he stopped walking. MaKayla was so lost in thought, she almost ran into him.

"What?" MaKayla was suddenly hot from embarrassment... and staring at Cain's body.

"Why are you pointing your flashlight at...me?" he asked over his shoulder.

"What are you talking about?" MaKayla laughed it off, playing it cool, terrible at acting like always. "I'm not."

"You're doing it right now," he said, matter-of-factly.

And oops, he was right. The circle of her beam encompassed the buns rounding out Cain's back pockets. Immediately, she jerked the flashlight somewhere, anywhere else, and landed on the tall wooden double doors set into the stone wall.

After a judgy glare, Cain went to the doors, operating the oversized iron lock with a combination of keys and twisting of cylinders.

It was cold down here at the bottom of the stairwell, and it felt damp, although MaKayla could see that the stones and grout were all dry. A smell at the cusp of mildew or rot battled a dry, dusty scent.

With a series of bulky clicking sounds and squeaky-hinged whines, Cane lifted a bar that acted as the ancient doors' knob. Putting those V-shaped muscles to work, he pulled each door open. The smell of dry dust chased any trace of must away. Warm light brushed her cheeks. She practically floated in past Cain.

Each wall was lined with shelves that either held rows of books lined up or triangular cubbies holding scrolls. And all of the wooden shelves were accented with silver and gold cherubic figures, gazing wistfully at their tomes.

Each stone corner had either a small fireplace, stove, or chimenea, spreading warmth everywhere and dancing rays of orange light scattering about. On stone pedestals stood sculpture, statue, and bust, and along the walls hung inset portraiture and landscape.

The first shelves she approached were dated reference books from cities like Pompeo, Roanoke, Serjilla, Constantinople, and tons of others she didn't recognize or languages she didn't speak.

One long wall was full of small cubbies, a puzzle of triangles of various sizes fitting together in a non-repeating geometric pattern. Scrolls within each triangle were wrapped in leathers and furs, others were in modern cardboard tubes or even hard plastic cases. One was in simple cellophane wrapping, and MaKayla couldn't help herself, reaching for it before turning to Cain to seek permission.

Without words, Cain must have understood her and dipped that sleek chin of his in a nod.

She pulled it out carefully, finding the paper springing open as soon as it cleared the cubby. Nice paper, close to thick photograph stock. It was a map, a printing of something once hand made. The words in the key and the title were in a foreign language, other characters mixed in with the alphabet she knew. Then she saw a name she recognized: Atlantis.

She couldn't help but laugh.

"It's real?"

"Something that mapmaker called Atlantis was real. Or else it wouldn't be here. We could look it up?"

It was so tempting. "Not now. First, show me about being a Fate."

He didn't reply but walked past her, his hand lightly brushing against her own as he went beyond a shelf and turned. Following along, she kept an eye on his lean figure as he snaked his way through a labyrinth of bookcases and stone walls.

On Cain walked, deeper into the maze, perpetually well-lit and warmed by the various fires set in corners. He confidently strode with long legs, knowing the way, leaving an uncertain MaKayla further and further behind. Pretty soon, she was barely getting a glimpse of a sliver of him before he'd disappear behind the next turn. She couldn't get lost here; it would be the end of her.

She thought back to remember the way she'd come already, but she hadn't been paying attention to landmarks. She panicked. The room got hot; the fires were too bright. She ran after Cain, one turn, then another, and then.

Where had he gone? There were four possible bookcases and one wall of model tall ships, but where was Cain? The longer MaKayla took to decide, the further into the maze Cain would go, the more turns he'd make, the more hopelessly lost she'd become.

"MaKayla, come on." Cain's head peeked out at a goofy angle from behind a bookshelf she hadn't even noticed.

She exhaled and felt a dumb smile she couldn't stop slowly spread across her face. Cain's smile was goofy too.

"I wasn't about to have you gawk at my backside the entire way through such a holy place as this library." Cain smirked.

Chapter 11

MaKayla

"So, who did the forbidding?"

"Kings, emperors, presidents, governors, mayors, sheriffs, pharaohs, etcetera. The *library's* not forbidden, you know." His chuckle embarrassed her.

"I know, man," she struck him on the arm. Pretty hard, maybe too hard. Great, now she was more embarrassed. "I just thought it would have been forbidden by like God or, I don't know...wizards?"

She tried to laugh it off, but his face said he was serious.

"MaKayla, there's something you should know, something I have to confess." His crystal blue eyes looked deep into hers, his jaw flexing with intensity. "I am a Reaper—"

"What, like a Grim Reaper?"

"Well, yeah, but that's not the confess—"

"That makes so much sense! A Grim Reaper and a Fate paired up like this." Realizations hit her suddenly, that he's killed, that in all mythology, Fates killed too. So maybe this guy, this adorable and ridiculous, tall, goth, and handsome guy was her partner in a long life of grim work. Eyes wide, she struggled for words and stuttered, working hard to stay honest and not try to lie, "But that's unbelievable."

"Believe it."

"I do! I totally do! But it's still unbelievable. So, when are you going to start teaching me to...kill people? Because, uh...Cain, I don't know if I can kill anyone."

"I'm not—I wouldn't ask you to kill anyone ever."

"Okay. Promise?" She took a step toward him, like she could get closer to the truth the closer she got to him.

But he didn't back away. In fact, he took a step toward her. "I promise."

"Okay." She could feel the heat of his body.

"I haven't been *assigned* to you," he assured her gently. His voice was deep and soft when he wanted it to be. His breath smelled like mint and faintly of coffee. "...If that was what you thought it was. We aren't like..."

"Coworkers for all of eternity?"

And they found themselves holding each other, or at least close enough to be touching bodies, hands up almost defensively up, resting on his chest. The feel of him, the tactile confirmation that he was real and so close to her, the contact sent a thrill from her palm throughout her body.

She looked up at him, his full lips, his broad chest lifting with breath, clear eyes looking down at her with ease, with care, and without judgment. She reached up and moved in, ready for her lips to close in on his. But he didn't hold her gaze. "That's all I got."

She laughed at the thought. A Grim Reaper, this eternal being of countless forms which could travel multiple planes of existence, talking to her in a Library of Forbidden Knowledge, presenting himself like 'that's all I got.'

She chuckled as she moved in for a kiss, whispering, "It's enough."

But he walked off.

And MaKayla almost fell over.

Cain

Cain stepped into the anteroom to present the two door-tables filled with tomes and scrolls, and MaKayla stumbled in behind, having lost her footing for some reason.

Cain knew the stones of these floors like the freckles on his arm, and there was nothing to trip on, but MaKayla was still so human. It was actually endearing. There was something so honest about being a silly human tripping your way through life.

But once she caught her bearings, she was impressed. "I love these tables."

"I don't know. They're weird to have around growing up. Seeing a normal dinner table on television really blew my mind."

"Is this…" MaKayla stood enamored in front of an illustrated story on a leather scroll, taking up more than half of one table. "An original ancient Greek document?"

"I'm pretty sure it's Phoenician," he shrugged. "But it's at least three thousand years old."

"That's well-made leather. What does it say?"

"Do you want me to translate, or the library can—"

"The library can…?"

He shrank a little, his attempt at showing off his linguistic skills rejected. But demonstrating the library's abilities was also a show of prowess. So, he summoned the Whispers.

"What are they?" MaKayla asked, her fingertips passing through one of the wisps of spirit and light.

"Seekers of knowledge," one whispered.

"Scholars," hissed another.

"Endless thirst for understanding."

MaKayla cleared her throat, somehow unaffected by the appearance of the floating transparent spirits, easily commanding their attention. "And what does this say?" She pointed at the scroll. The Whispers answered in succession.

"The quest of Orpheus."

"Live man escaped to the underworld."

"He sought to overturn a death."

"Through an evil magic, he cheated the Fates."

"Thrice."

"What does it say about the Fates?"

"Women."

"Sisters."

"One spinning thread."

"One to measure."

"One to cut."

"But Orpheus patched a thread."

"Only a Fate can patch a thread."

"And the Fates railed."

"And the Fates drew a thread."

"And the Fates cut."

"Cut Orpheus down."

"Well. That wasn't in the version I read." MaKayla shivered. "What else does it say about Fates?"

The Whispers had nothing left to say and floated about

awkwardly. Of course, MaKayla couldn't have known that, and just as she opened her mouth to speak, one of the Whispers whimpered, "One to cut."

Another randomly wailed, "Orpheus cheated the Fates."

"Okay." MaKayla caught on. "What else? What's the next book?"

"So, you're a Reaper," one Whisper said spookily.

A bubbling, joyful chuckle came out of a broad, natural smile. MaKayla laughed, and Cain couldn't help but join her.

He'd been poring over these books all week, pushing himself, focused on reading and rereading to decipher important details. He'd stayed up late and given himself headaches from reading in bad light. But with MaKayla, it was easy, light, fun. Even this aggravating research was enjoyable with her.

They went through two more books with her asking questions of the Whispers and cracking jokes. Once, their hands touched as they leaned over a painting of the Ancient Fates. Cain recoiled; his cheeks warmed. MaKayla kept her hand there but visibly blushed.

Why wasn't she afraid of him? Why hadn't things drastically changed after admitting what he was? How could she look him dead in the eyes, smile, and just melt him into a blathering, very human boy?

When she'd exhausted the books Cain found, she asked, "So how do we find more?"

"Good luck. I've exhausted this place, asking about Fates, lovelines, and heartstrings."

"Is there an old computer somewhere to search a database? Or books to tell me where the books are?"

"You can simply ask."

"This feels an awful lot like those home computers you call

by their first name with their soft lady robot voices."

They laughed easily, freely, without a care in the world. The guy who had one day left to take a power-imbued soul and the god-powered girl who knew nothing about herself or her powers.

"Hello, library?" she giggled adorably. "Can you find information on the following subjects: the three sisters, three Greek sisters, sister spins, sister measures, sister cuts, goddess spins measures cuts thread, sisters destiny, sisters shears, and who Orpheus cheated."

Wow, this girl was smart. No, he had to stop thinking of her as a girl when it was becoming more and more obvious that she was something more.

As the Whispers set to work, the library groaned to life, the air moving, the fires flaring, and the books seemed to stretch and flex as if the place were breathing. And the girl with shears of Fate sheathed to her leg bounced giddily.

Again, Cain damned himself for lying to her, for using her.

"MaKayla, I really do need to tell you the truth. Not that I'm a Reaper—that's not the confession. I just owed you that fact, too. The truth is, I lied. I don't know anything about Fates."

"That's obvious, Cain." she giggled and shrugged. She gave him a quick look up and down while awaiting the Whispers' return. In that quick look, she devoured him, judging every inch of him and responding with only a flirty smirk. There on the library floor, he felt like that look had crumpled him up and tossed him somewhere near the wastebasket.

"No, I need to tell you...I have to say what I was planning, what I was going to do."

"Hold up there, man. It's no big reveal that you're not the greatest teacher or the most knowledgeable in my particular subject. But you don't need to tell me or admit or confess anything. I know you don't want to admit you make mistakes because you're human, but you should really think about forgiving yourself every once in a while."

"Forgive myself?"

"Yes. Especially when you want to whip yourself about something you've already decided not to go through with it. See a problem, make a change, forgive yourself, and move on."

"You make it sound so simple."

"It's not. At first. It's like anything—you've got to practice and get good at it."

The irony of the student teaching the mentor was just too much for Cain. But he wanted to listen. He wanted to believe her, believe that he could forgive himself and move on. It was too much, and words just burst out of him. "I'm a terrible Reaper. My parents are going to make me stay human because if I mess up, all of life and death gets out of balance. And I know I can handle it, but simultaneously I can't. And I'm scared. And I don't know why I just said all that. I know *why* I said it, it's true, but I don't know why I felt the need to tell you."

"Okay."

"I'm sorry."

"I've got nothing to forgive you for. Forgive yourself. You want to talk about it?"

"No." But he did. Like the jumble of words lodged in his chest, burning to be spoken. But she didn't want to hear apologies from him. So he didn't say any more about it.

"Oh, before I forget, I got this for you." And she tossed him a small purple box, which he easily caught.

"What is this?"

"Open it."

"You got this for me?"

"It's nothing special. Open it."

What was the last gift he got from someone who wasn't his parents? Maybe a birthday party at twelve? Thirteen? Fewer and fewer people would attend them each year until attendees were down to the single digits, including parents.

This gift was an instantly precious object. The purple wrapping was soft to the touch and stretchy. Purple with black designs, a fat purple and black knot pulled easily to release a long black ribbon. The wrapping was a large square cloth which fell open to drape over this hand. "What's this?"

"It's a bandana." She pulled it from his hand and wrapped it once around his wrist, then tied a loose knot. "The goth look is flat unless you have a splash of color to emphasize all the black."

He looked in the mirror, admiring how the deep purple stood out, making the rest of his outfit seem even bleaker. She was right, smiling her closed-lip I-told-you-so smirk. She was short next to him, bouncy where he was stolid. Her cheeks had tan tones where he was pink with red blotches, inviting features that pulled him down to her where he looked like an overbearing fragile vase on a pedestal, top-loaded and looking down on others. Everything about her was warm and welcoming, but they looked good together. She made him look less ridiculous in their awkward human teen getups.

He still had the small box to open, which held a plastic popping hand fidgeter—yet another treasure. She had spent time thinking of him while he wasn't around. Not because she needed anything from him; just because she was thinking of him.

And he had planned on using her for her powers. Again,

the immense guilt struck. Images of a hurt, sad, or angry MaKayla flashed in his mind. What was it she said, though? Self-forgiveness? He tried deep breaths, silently forgiving himself with each exhale. He loosened up each time he breathed out until he was relaxed again, although the feeling of guilt was still there, just deeper inside. Tucked away.

"It's just a fidget popper; it's not that big a deal," MaKayla said lightly.

Cain snapped out of his self-reflective trance back to see the cute couple in the mirror—MaKayla and Cain, complementary opposites. The guy in the reflection was happy.

"I really like it. Thanks."

"That's the nicest thing you've ever said to me," she replied softly, reaching down for his hand.

They did look good as a couple. And they both knew he couldn't really train her anymore. As the Whispers filled the tables with books, tablets, and scrolls, Cain stood frozen as the beautiful Fate girl reached down to hold his hand. He took a breath. This was it. This was going to be his first kiss.

It wouldn't technically be his first kiss; he'd kissed Carla Walters in middle school, but they didn't really like each other; they were just bored and curious. This would be a first real kiss; meaningful and vulnerable. An expression of thought and care, mutual respect and safety.

He reached back for her hand and turned to face her.

He leaned down for her face.

She looked down as she grabbed him by the wrist.

He chuckled a bit. Her going to hold his hand while he went in for a kiss; they couldn't be more like clumsy young lovers. He tipped her chin to bring her face to his, to press his mouth to hers, to connect with a kiss...

"No, let me." She grunted as her hand slipped from his.

She looked up suddenly, her forehead connecting with his chin and lip.

"Oof," went Cain.

"Ow!" said MaKayla. She rubbed her forehead.

He touched a finger to his chin, then checked his lip. Blood.

"I was going to show you the bandana also works around your neck." She held up the cloth wrapping for the present, which she'd untied from his wrist; it was not an attempt to hold his hand.

"Sorry. I thought you..." Cain didn't know how to end that sentence.

"Wanted to make out?" She continued pressing on her forehead; Cain's chin did jut out, and man, it must have been sharp.

"No, I thought..." Again, he had no idea where that sentence was going.

"What time is it?" she asked, then kept on without waiting for an answer. "I should probably get going."

They left, awkwardly, back out of the Library of Forbidden Knowledge, up flights and flights of stone stairs, and up out of the Morrigan's basement.

They were immediately hit with the smell of bacon.

"Great news, kid!" Cain's mom whispered as she rushed from the kitchen. "Your father's home!"

She came around the corner in a house dress, complete with an apron and wooden spoon, just to come face to face with MaKayla Colfax.

"Who are you, and what are you doing in my house?" The tiny woman let out a deep growl, awaiting an answer.

Chapter 12

MaKayla

"**M**om, this is MaKayla..."

Cain's mom gawked at him, polite fake smile still spread wide, showing perfect white teeth, but her angry eyes were blankly expectant, unsatisfied with Cain's answer.

MaKayla stood in the middle of some argument she didn't understand.

Cain shot a desperate, angry look at his mother. "She's a friend from school."

This gave his mom pause. Her voice dropped even lower as she echoed, "A friend from school...like *a friend*?"

MaKayla wasn't certain what distinction was being made right then.

"Yeah, Mom. She's just a friend." Cain pouted, rolling his eyes. It was cute.

She raised an eyebrow, "But a *friend* friend?"

Still, MaKayla didn't exactly follow, but she was pretty sure she was being called a slut.

"She's just a friend."

"And I've got to get home and work on an art project," MaKayla added with a sugary sweet fake smile.

"Nonsense. Stay for dinner. It's been so long since Cain brought a...friend home."

"She really has to go, Mom."

"Sorry, Mrs. Morrigan, I really need to go work on—"

"Nonsense," a gruff, low voice boomed from further down the hall. "Stay. And after dinner, it's family game night."

"Father, you're home?" Cain's face quirked in confusion.

A thick, muscled, pinker version of Cain stepped from around the corner. He bulged with mass like he was stretching his skin as much as his blue button up shirt and khaki shorts. His eyes had an intense stare with a sickly redness to them. His enormous nostrils flexed open further as he inhaled, sucking in air and all of the energy in the hall. His smile was a sneer of too-large white teeth. But his hulking mass was ridiculous, wrapped in a blue and white striped apron and poofy chef's hat. A lion dressed up as a clown.

He held up flour-powdered hands, wiggling thick, stubby fingers. "And it's breakfast for dinner."

MaKayla always thought of herself as a brave woman, never shirking from fear, but she felt herself scooting over to Cain, almost behind him.

While his dad didn't even acknowledge MaKayla's presence, Cain shielded her, pressing against his dad's stare as if it carried a force with it, pushing Cain back. There was an electric intensity between the two of them. Of course there was no force, none that MaKayla could see, but his father's stare still bested Cain, visibly humbled him. His shoulders and back tensed harder and harder, drawing him into a slouch, pulling him into a cower, curling him back into what was a disgusting subservience.

Was this the expression of an abusive relationship? Was this a toxic home life that shaped Cain?

But it never escalated, as Mr. Morrigan went back to the kitchen and Mrs. Morrigan switched over to hostess responsibilities. "Can I get you something to drink, MaKayla? Cain, get your guest a drink, don't be rude. MaKayla, do you have any allergies or foods to avoid, kosher? Gluten-free? Vegan?"

"I don't think pineapple should be on pizza, but that's it. I'll take some water."

"There are people who do that?"

"Bad people."

"I'm glad you joined us, MaKayla. Ice in that water?"

"Whatever's easy."

Sitting across a table from Cain's father was not easy.

"I want to hear about this art project," Mrs. Morrigan announced with teasing excitement.

MaKayla smiled back politely and tried to engage with Cain's mom, but she could barely keep her eyes off his dad. The man's presence was so unsettling. He had implacable violent and cruel qualities about him, although MaKayla couldn't describe what about his look or demeanor conveyed that. In fact, objectively, the man was ignoring her, zoning out, staring at his own plate. But as far as MaKayla was concerned, he was coiled, drawn, loaded, ready to strike.

So she answered the questions directed at her, dividing her attention between her polite hostess and dangerous weapon of an adult at the other end of the table. "It's a collage piece; I've been doing a collage series this whole year."

"Oh? Is there a particular subject matter, or is this non-objective art?"

"Mo-*om*, leave her alone. MaKayla works on this project for like three hours a day during the week. I'm sure she doesn't want to talk about it out of school."

"It's okay," she smiled. It was nice to have somebody sticking up for her. At home, she was always standing up for herself because there was no way Dad or Aaron would stand up to Mom. Plus, no one at home knew anything about her art or art in general. "I put real-world subjects in abstract settings. Where did you learn about non-objective art?"

"Oh, I studied art for hundreds of years."

Silver utensils clattered on plates, sending bits of egg and pancake up from Cain's father's plate. He just glared even harder at the center of the table, focusing immense frustration at one square inch between the salt and pepper. He stopped chewing and Mrs. Morrigan froze.

She tittered a fake laugh at everyone at the table, shrugging. "Well, it felt like hundreds of years. What is the subject matter of your newest collage?"

"A girl. A hero. But she was lied to about her journey and winds up sacrificing much more than she'd anticipated."

"Wow. How old are you again, MaKayla?"

"Seventeen."

"Has anyone ever told you you're an old soul?"

At this, Mr. Morrigan huffed a sneer of a laugh. Simultaneously, he appeared glossed over but also was obviously paying enough attention to disapprove of what was being said.

"People say I'm mature for my age?" MaKayla answered peppily, doing what she could to keep the conversation light.

"MaKayla's going to have to leave right after dinner," Cain suddenly announced with a nervous quality MaKayla wasn't used to. Without looking up from overly-syruped pancakes, he went on, "She can't stay for games."

"Nonsense, I'm sure MaKayla can play a couple before she leaves."

Before MaKayla could answer, Cain took a hard line. "No, her collage is due soon."

Then Mr. Morrigan spoke, again addressing the entire room without looking at anyone. "Games are important, and you're not getting out of them, young man."

Was Cain just using her as an excuse to skip out on family game night? Admittedly, the idea of the Morrigans, complete with two sullen guys and one perky woman, playing colorful, fun children's games was a little laughable. She couldn't picture Cain squealing "Yahtzee" with joy or having a laugh about losing a round of Go-Fish.

Her curiosity got the better of her. Though it was obvious Cain had done his best to keep his parents off her back and maybe accidentally discovering that she was a rookie Fate having dinner with three undercover Grim Reapers, she *had* to see what a Morrigan game night was like.

"I could stay for a game or two," MaKayla shrugged and smiled sheepishly, enjoying a bite of omelet.

Cain fumed silently for the rest of the meal. Later in the kitchen, the two helped clean up while Cain's parents set up in the other room.

"This is the worst idea ever," Cain said with so much panic in his whisper, it was a squeak.

MaKayla was obviously enjoying herself, nonchalantly scraping plates off into the trash, sucking in her cheeks to keep from smiling.

He handed her all of the serving utensils, cleared his throat, and said in a lower, more composed tone, "I'll text you seven minutes in. Pretend it's an emergency with your family, and I'll walk you out."

She stopped accepting dirty dishes to soak in the sink and folded her arms across her chest. Leaning back on herself, she raised one thick eyebrow. "What games does your dad like to play?"

Cain turned into a cartoon, and his eyeballs bulged out of his head. "What? What does that even mean? You're not going to find out. You'll never find out; you'll never know! You have to leave."

"Just stop it, okay? Whatever bad thing you think is going to happen isn't, okay? Besides, I don't think you're as worried about me getting found out as you are about being embarrassed of your family. Well, get over it. Everybody's family is embarrassing."

The words hung heavily in the air. She didn't want to push him too hard. She didn't want to say the next logical point, that no matter how much he claimed to hate humans, he was acting like one. And no matter how much he wanted her to think of herself as superhuman, she was human, too. Seeing Cain like this, his calm, too-cool veneer dropped, his voice rushed and high-pitched with worry, his bravado crumbling as things got out of control...it was hot. He was hot.

And thinking about him got her hot.

Suddenly, as he pouted about her words, she decided to act. She leaned, closed her eyes, and connected.

Lips to lips. Electricity and magic and a rush of feelings, but then...he kissed back.

He was tall and strong and forceful in ways she didn't expect or know she wanted. He was eager, overpowering, and voracious. His lips tasted like maple syrup, and he smelled like a sweet vanilla musk. He pulled her close, and his arms cradled her back.

This wasn't kissing a boy in middle school. This was taking a leap of faith, blindly putting herself into the unknown to kiss someone and then getting kissed back, getting romanced... getting really turned on.

"Are you two okay? It's awful quiet in there!" Mrs. Morrigan called from the living room.

MaKayla dropped the silverware with a loud clatter. Cain smiled bigger than she'd ever seen.

Cain

He couldn't stop smiling, and frankly, it was pissing him off. How on Earth could MaKayla Colfax be so damned enchanting that he was relaxed and grinning through a family game night? Floating ten feet above the rest of the room (and he kept checking that that wasn't doing so literally), his usual anxiety around Father had subsided, or rather, Cain had risen above it. Even Mom's overt attempts to befriend MaKayla weren't riling him.

"You're awfully good at this, MaKayla," Mom said in disbelief as she joined her son in bankruptcy.

Father exhaled a disapproving grunt.

"My family's pretty competitive. Plus, as the older sister, I have to stay ahead of my brother, and he's a smart kid."

Half an hour later, MaKayla was just as chipper, and Father was even quieter and more desperate. Still, he pretended to ignore her, to focus on the game in front of him. Cain knew he didn't mean to be insulting; it was just how his father was: terrible with people.

He was always too intense; vocally, physically, even his facial expressions screamed "intense." But thankfully, either MaKayla didn't notice, or she used it to fuel her impressive game play.

Mom sighed heavily. "So, I guess we'll call it a draw and move onto the next game?"

"I've never not won," Father grumbled, either back to Mom or to himself. By then, his chin was pushing his hands into the tabletop, as if a closer view could show him a way to defeat MaKayla.

She let out a heavy sigh and offered, "Maybe I take pics of where we are and you and I can finish this game some other time, Mr. Morrigan?"

"Deal," he said, looking up at her with his devilishly intense smile he always gets when he makes plans to play a game.

She'd somehow handled him perfectly. Father was...delicate. His feelings were easily hurt while at the same time he was stubborn and competitive. But with grace and ease, MaKayla had handled him. Was there anything she couldn't do?

The next game was charades, and that ended up being something MaKayla couldn't do. She and Cain lost handily to Mom and Father, but it was good-hearted. Everybody had fun, there was some laughter all the way to tears at some point. It was easy.

Again, Cain was floating. Was this even reality? He had feelings for someone who had feelings back. She kissed him. Were they going to start dating? Was he going to be excited about going to school now?

And Mom and Father were obviously over the moon about

her, even though Father was a bit too awkward to express it. But everyone wanted to walk MaKayla out at the end of the evening; everyone crowded into the slender hallway, including hulking Father. He helped her into her heavy fur-lined coat, then extended a hand, putting together a pretty normal and not-too-intense smile.

"Miss MaKayla, it's been a pleasure having you over. I look forward to finishing our game."

"Thank you, Mr. Morrigan." She took his hand.

Things happened when Father shook a human's hand. Usually, he got a sense of them or at least their relationship with Death. But if Death was near, sometimes the handshake recipient would catch some odd vibes. A big reason Father came across as so skittish and intense was how difficult it was for him to not constantly siphon information. He had to take care how he interacted—not too much eye contact and never any accidental physical contact. But this was different; he was meeting a girl Cain was interested in. At least that's what Cain thought. It was more likely that Father hadn't thought too much of the gesture either.

But Father's eyes popped wide. He froze, his lip quivering. The expression was unmistakable.

Fear.

Immediately, tears rolled down the big man's cheeks as he fell to his knees. He was still holding her hand, and he pressed his forehead to it.

"Sister," he said in a reverent whisper as if afraid of the power from giving his voice to such a name. "Sister Fate, I had no idea. Please believe me."

What was happening to Father?

And his saucer-sized wet eyes shone up again. Father was

pouring sweat now, eyes up at MaKayla, silently begging. Worshiping.

With his free hand he waved to his family to kneel. Mom immediately supplicated, closing her eyes and spreading her hands. Baffled, Cain scrunched his thick eyebrows incredulously and gave a little crouch.

MaKayla's mouth hung open, shaping the beginnings of words that she never spoke.

Father said hurriedly, as if to plead before she could speak, "If my family or I have offended you tonight, I am gravely sorry. We will stop at nothing to rectify our wrongs."

MaKayla's eyes pleaded with Cain's, but he could only shrug in answer.

Father whispered back angrily, "Cain, kneel! Show respect!"

Cain stood still, baffled by his father's behavior.

Mom chided in an even tone, eyes still closed, "Cain, listen to your father."

"Sh!"

Tone still calm, Mom warned Father, "Stanley, don't shush me."

"Deb, don't serve a superior being breakfast for dinner."

"I didn't know what was going on, Stanley. I still don't. And you *love* breakfast for dinner."

"What is going on is Cain invited an esteemed Sister Fate into our home."

Mom opened her eyes and said to her son in that self-satisfied way a parent who's been listened to says, "You found a Fate for your assignment?"

"What assignment?" MaKayla looked at Cain, trying to keep up.

"Cain needs help with a soul?" Father asked.

But Cain's eyes were locked with MaKayla's.

"What soul?" she asked, a sparkle of a tear forming in one eye.

He wished they were alone, he wished he could explain everything without showing Father what an absolute screw-up he was. He wished he'd told her earlier.

"Is this true, Cain?" Father asked.

Mom asked something, too, but Cain didn't hear. He couldn't hear anything. He could only see MaKayla: in pain, hurt by a lie, stabbed by a weapon of his own making. He could only feel icy guilt, hot shame, and the sting of a heart too uncertain to keep feeling.

"I'm sorry," Cain's voice croaked. There was more to say. There were more words to that sentence, but he never got to voice them.

She ran out into the thick, snowy night.

Chapter 13

MaKayla

Reading thousand-year-old manuscripts before crying all night probably didn't help, but MaKayla woke up feeling puffy, gross, and hopeless.

She lay there in the blinding light of the late morning, watching the endless parade of dust motes in the morning sun, its brightness amplified by a couple feet of snow. Sadness from just about everything had somehow combined with exhaustion, and the concoction coursed through her body; filling her muscles, soaking into her bones, marinating her brain.

Parsing out what was real in her life from what was a lie was now an impossible task. She had graduated from a lying mother to a lying boy. Everyone had a turn using MaKayla for whatever they needed. And now here she was, dried and wrung out, with no truth of her own to hold onto, only half-truths from the people using her.

And of course, there were about a million texts from Cain, checking on her, insisting they talk, then immediately apologizing for their tone. She left them unanswered as he continued his single-sided conversation. He was the last person she wanted to see, even if she wanted to—no, had to— had an absolute compulsion to find out simply why. Why had he used her like that? Why was the concept of asking for help so absolutely foreign to this boy that he'd rather spend a week keeping up an intricate web of lies? Why did he kiss her back if it was all a lie?

She had too many questions and too many texts but an absolute revulsion at the thought of resolving all of them.

But she could resolve some of them.

The house was empty. Notes and more texts explained that Dad and Aaron were headed for the big sled hill, which would keep them occupied into the afternoon. Obviously, Dad was trying to make Mom's moving out easier on Aaron.

If that even what was happening. Yesterday's meeting with Mom had been more cryptic warning than actual communication of their current situation.

MaKayla got out cereal, milk, and a bowl, then thought better of it and texted her mom for brunch.

They decided on a brewery, trendy and lined with ship lap, and met within the hour.

Mom hated the cocktails there, but still ordered three. The drinking made the admissions come easier. But this was no interrogation. The moment they were left alone by the waitstaff, MaKayla sat back and said simply, "The only way we leave this meal with any kind of relationship is if you spill it. All of it."

And honestly, more was spilled than MaKayla was prepared.

"So, Dad doesn't know anything. That was always our deal: no questions about the past. Twenty-twenty hindsight—not the best foundation for a marriage. But it's hard. Marriage is hard, any marriage, I'm sure. But ours is complicated. The handgun is nowhere near the biggest blow-up, believe me. I've gotten your father angry..."

The server came by, and they ordered food; her mother got another drink.

"Your grandmother... I didn't have a childhood like you, MaKayla. Now, I don't mean that as a guilt trip for giving you and Aaron such a great life. I mean, I didn't have a childhood like you did. I had training. Preparation. I was raised and told that I would have to fight forces of evil and chaos. Even before I got my scissors. I memorized lists upon lists of gods and goddesses, stories about the beginnings of the world, prophecies about the end. Your grandmother believed that the power of three united Fates could challenge any god and rightfully should. And she said we were the gods' end. And that was my childhood and my relationship with my mom. And this is not a guilt trip or anything." She was crying at this point but quieted down under the dabbing of a white cloth napkin. Her drinks were swapped out by the waitress.

"Another please," she asked quietly. Once the server left, she cleared her throat and said, "I did not want anything like that for you. So I pushed in the other direction. I pushed for a simple, quiet life. And I pushed you. Because I was afraid of the day your scissors would show up. So I kept mine close, next to a handgun. I still have all the training and the knowledge, MaKayla. If that's something you want, I can give it to you now. But without all of the trauma and abuse, you know."

Her mom expected a yes. MaKayla knew gratitude was expected, maybe an apology. some gesture to acknowledge her mother's sacrifices. But MaKayla wasn't budging.

"I don't trust you."

"Buttercup, everything I just said is true."

MaKayla had to force herself to speak, knowing each word harmed her mother, but knowing MaKayla had to protect herself. "That may be, but I can't trust you any more. I can only assume everything you say is a way to gain pity or to guilt me. This whole 'I had such an awful childhood' story might be true, but you're only telling me a a means to stay in my life."

That shut her mom up, who now only looked down at her food.

"I don't need the Mom I had. I don't need someone second-guessing me, or criticizing how I look, or giving gifts just for the expectation of having a parade thrown for being a better mother than she had. You may have had a bad childhood, but I didn't do that to you and I owe you nothing for it."

Her mom was crying now. And if MaKayla thought about it too much, she'd be crying, too. So she kept on, "You're my mom, and I love you, but I don't need you. And I definitely don't need you using your knowledge of the shears or whatever diablerie is as a way to control me. I'd like us to have a relationship. But until you can prove to me it's not for your benefit, it's going to go how I say it's going to go."

"MaKayla, it's not like you're an adult, you can't just-"

"You can have a daughter who silently hates you on weekends and holidays, or whatever you and Dad work out, or you can respect the fact that I'm giving you a shot. That's your decision to make."

Her mom's silence gave the answer.

"If we do this, it's my way. I'll contact you with a subject, something supernatural. You write down everything you remember, give me the time and space to review the notes, then we meet on my terms to discuss. It's either that, or we never speak of this again."

MaKayla surprised herself at how emotionless the words came. She was feeling them, rushed full of anger and guilt, pushing back against the desire to hurt her mother now that she finally had an upper hand. But this wasn't revenge or retribution. This was a boundary. This was deal-making. And MaKayla knew she wasn't willing to give any more, to sacrifice any part of herself, to budge that boundary an inch.

Mom must have known it too, answering, voice quivering, "Whatever you want, baby."

"I do love you, Mom, but no mentoring here. No protecting me. No pushing."

"I promise, buttercup. I love you, too."

The food came: Mom's pancakes and eggs, which just reminded MaKayla of dinner at the Morrigan's the night before. A juicy, rare steak for MaKayla. Once they were alone again, she cut a thick bite of pink beef and said, "Start with telling me what you know about Grim Reapers."

Cain

He left the house early the next day, avoiding his parents. He drove out to the locks and walked around; the giant empty basins only made him feel colder and emptier.

Good. He deserved to feel cold and empty. He deserved to hurt for what he did to MaKayla. And then there was a moment. Looking over the old cold metal rails, down into the metal basins of an empty lock. Cain thought about going over, ending it. Ending this shame and embarrassment. The unfinished business of admitting his grave mistakes to his parents, and somehow, to MaKayla as well. This struggle to shed this disgusting humanity, this sickly and nasty human body that was capable of nothing but pain and cringe.

He even thought about calling 988, but then he wondered... If he did step out into nothing and fall in this human form, would Father have to come and harvest his soul? Is that what Cain wanted? To make his parents feel sorry? Just because they threatened to make him learn. Just because he hadn't been great at reaping.

Maybe they were right; maybe he should spend longer in training.

He didn't want to die. He just wanted to stop being such a disappointment to everyone.

He texted MaKayla again, ready to own up to everything. He texted his father, ready to ask for help.

He texted his mom, apologizing for ruining family game night.

Nobody got back to him.

He grabbed lunch, went back home to an empty house, and took his tacos down to the Library of Forbidden Knowledge. Her books were still out. The books she'd managed to seek out even though he'd been searching all week...even though he was the one who grew up using the library. Of course, MaKayla had found a way to mine more information. Of course, she found things in his own blind spots.

He really liked her. This wasn't teenage lust or some positional relationship. She was the best person he'd ever met. And he had to figure out how to make it up to her.

He texted a couple more times.

Then back to the books. Back to practice. Back to the plan; a new form, untested. Everything about this harvest was risky.

Okay, so the plan was a guaranteed failure. But he got himself into this mess. Unless his parents got back to him in time, he was going to get himself out of it.

There was one way he found. One form he could take that might have been powerful enough, sneaky enough to surprise old man Skelton. It was a long shot that he could even do it, but he had to try. This was how Cain got out of all this mess. Not suicide. Not giving up. He was going to harvest this soul by the assigned time, even if it was the most difficult metamorphosis a Reaper could attempt.

Again, he pored over the thousands-year-old tomes, warning him that only the most practiced of Reapers should attempt such a transformation.

MaKayla

MaKayla's dad and Aaron were still gone when she got home. The text messages were mounting, but by now, MaKayla was too nervous to answer. Between the little she learned about Reapers from the Morrigans and the limited scope of her mom's knowledge, MaKayla had pieced together that if Cain screwed this assignment up, the repercussions would change reality.

This was too big for her. Granted, everything that MaKayla had encountered over the last week had been too big, but this was different. The balance of life and death would be thrown out of whack. The laws of nature would be upended.

She rubbed the shears, snug in her thigh holster, but the comforting metal wasn't enough. She had to do something. If all of this was too big for her, it was definitely too big for Cain alone.

So she got out the phone and scrolled through Cain's texts.

Can we talk?

I owe you a real apology. You deserve to know the truth. If you don't want to meet, can we call?

The kiss was real, FYI.

Truth is a soul is tethered w a heartstring. I need a f8 to snip by midnight 2nite

I lied to you bc I'm a bad reapr. Wanted to show Dad I was ready, but I'm not.

I decided against using you and your (scissor emoji), then I got caught up in your self-forgiveness idea.

I'll never forgive myself for screwing up my only chance with you."

It hit hard. MaKayla was already ready to help, to volunteer to dig Cain out of this hole, to step in and help fix the entire world, despite the immensity of the task.

But as she formulated a response, the doorbell rang.

It couldn't be him...could it? She dashed downstairs. Were they so synced, was he so in her mind that he knew she'd eventually agree to help him out? She flung open the door. Would she be able to work alongside him without punching him in the mouth?

Shivering in the doorway, teary-eyed and makeup smudged, stood Ora. She was having trouble looking MaKayla in the eye.

"Can we talk?" Ora's voice was coarse and worn.

"Of course, come in. You want some tea?"

"You don't gotta be nice like that. I've been awful to you, M."

"Take off those wet clothes. Sit down and dry out."

The shift in focus came easily to MaKayla. She could deal with Cain and the world-ending drama later—they had until midnight, and Cain was definitely a procrastinator.

But a friend in pieces, that was immediate. This was someone MaKayla could help right here, right now. She warmed the kettle, readied the Colfax's funniest mugs, and started a small fire in the fireplace. Ora was still worked up. She sat on the couch and pulled a hoodie up and over herself to snuggle in.

By the time all of MaKayla's scurrying about was done, they were on opposite sides of the couch under heavy blankets, watching the fire and sipping steamy green mint tea. They sipped and made approving hums for a few moments. MaKayla waited until her friend was ready to start talking.

"Mark and I broke up." Ora began crying again.

MaKayla reached for her, but Ora waved her away. "No, no, it's alright. We were terrible for each other. This should have happened way earlier."

Guilt twisted like a dagger in MaKayla's side, and she wanted to admit her part in it: her delaying, procrastinating in helping a friend because MaKayla was in training. But how much could she even tell Ora? How much of the story of this week was remotely believable?

Besides, what Ora needed was someone to listen. So MaKayla did.

"It finally happened. I tried breaking up with him like a week ago, but he said he had a vision we were meant to be together. And I guess I didn't wanna push it. Well, Mark had another dream last night where we weren't together, and it convinced him. He was worried, convinced it was like some warning of bad things to come if we split up, but I saw an opening, and I pushed, and I didn't stop. We talked for like an hour and decided to try and be friends. But for real, like, try. So it's good, and I...I couldn't tell Mark, but...I cheated."

She broke out in tears again. This time, the two met in

the middle of the couch and shared a long cry. When Ora finally settled and had some more tea, she wiped her face, sniffing herself into presentability before saying, "And I was so miserable and took so much of it out on you, M."

"It's okay. I knew you were hurting. I forgive you."

The girls shared another long hug, followed by tissues and more tea. Ora was red-faced with a stuffy nose, but was visibly relieved.

"How about you? What's going on with Cain Morrigan?"

"What? Nothing. He was helping me with a thing."

"Okay, vagueries. Does he no longer help your thing?"

"We just have to finish it." MaKayla stared into the fire. She was procrastinating and she knew it. Yes, Ora needed her help, but Cain needed her, too. And now that this emergency of Ora's was manageable, it was on to the next one, the bigger one, the world-consuming emergency.

"In fact..." MaKayla pulled her phone out and replied to Cain. *"I'll do it. When and where?"*

She put her phone back, brushed the hair out of her face like checking another item off of a very stressful to-do list, and said, "But once this thing is over tonight, Cain won't be helping me anymore."

It was a pretty good line. The smirk MaKayla had was one of genuine surprise; she was never great at coming up with a perfect witticism. She sipped her tea with great satisfaction.

Ora arched an eyebrow. "If you say so, girl. But I hear Cain Morrigan is also helping Ivy Skelton with a thing."

MaKayla knew Ivy was trouble, trouble she'd been avoiding since their little gift-giving-gone-wrong. But she didn't know about Cain and her. Did this have something to do with Mark? Or was Ivy another girl Cain used to help him with his 'assignment'?

Ora went on, "And I can tell you things you wouldn't believe about Ivy Skelton."

"Please, do tell."

Cain

By now, Cain had scoped out the hospital and its parking lot thoroughly.

He'd parked at the baseball fields, then dissipated into mist to reform at the edge of the hospital parking lot. Cars were coming in for the third shift, familiar cars stopping as steamy-headed people got out with their coffees and cigarettes, finishing both before heading inside.

There was something unsettling about a surprise late snow in spring. People had to get winter coats back out of storage, since their bodies had adjusted to warmer temperatures. But there was something dangerous in the air when it snowed after Easter; it was supposed to be closer to July than January. It was almost dishonest of Mother Nature, or maybe She was just acting out.

And the weather had been relentless for over two days now; it kept everyone on edge and off guard in the quiet cold, unending piles of snow absorbing sound but amplifying all light, making any decently lit parking lot at night as bright as daylight.

The late snow had disturbed Lockport. People trickled in late everywhere because of road conditions because the snowplows weren't ready to go this late in the season. Walking paths had now been stomped down into solid, slick ice. Puffy-coated people aligned and waddled like penguins down organically twisting pathways leading out of the parking lot and into the hospital. And still, more snow fell.

Cain carefully identified each waddler heading inside. There were three sets of two nurses who'd be working the third shift on the fourth floor, two of them rotating. One janitor. Based on his surveillance, there were about five nurses he'd feel comfortable taking; as in they didn't seem like they'd put up too much of a fight but also weren't too old. And only one janitor fit the criteria.

There wasn't really math involved. Cain only hoped he'd be dealing with one of the six hospital workers he'd scoped out this week. And then he saw his target: the young janitor. Perfect.

He checked the time, hoping again for a message from either parent and was again tempted to respond to MaKayla's texts.

Of course. The one person he wanted to keep safe and clear of this mess wanted to help. And the two beings he needed help from were unavailable for the first time in known history.

He ran through his head every step of the plan, every warning from the ancient books (excluding the warnings to never attempt), took a deep breath, and converted to his shadow form.

As the young janitor tossed an empty coffee cup into recycling and entered the hospital, the shadow of fear that was now Cain Morrigan slid across the snowy parking lot, unsettling the landscape of perfect white. The patch of faded darkness crossed the patch of snowed-upon grass, through the brick building exterior, and inside.

The darkness of the janitor's closet was comforting to Cain the shadow. He pooled in the corner underneath a shelf, safe from the slits of harsh lighting coming through the closet door's blinds. The hospital was always a rush of noises. Incessant beeping came from all rooms, the tapping of fingers on keyboards, chatter of coworkers, and underneath it all, every so often, cries of pain. A patient called out in the darkness, uncertain of where they were. Someone under the influence screamed in frustration, tied to their bed with tubes and stickers.

A sudden swell of confidence hit him. The hospital was Death's domain. The thin veneer of human life was nearly transparent here. While Cain had to be cognizant to the call of Death to be sure he didn't run into his father, he still felt the power of Death, the residual spiritual energy of passing that existed within the hospital walls.

The plan could work. He could do this; ancient texts be damned.

A loud voice, masculine and overly friendly, called out from right outside the doorway. The electric door-locking mechanism beeped. The door handle shook.

Now or never.

Cain stepped out of himself, one of his more terrifying forms emerging from another. He transformed. The Crow-Beast Cain walked out of his own shadow as if the dark puddle were a hole leading to a staircase in the floor. Crow-Beast's feathers were purplish black, numbering in the thousands, laying flat and perfect, a completed jigsaw puzzle that pierced the skin. And Crow-Beast felt each piece, each feather. He stood, taller and taller, nearly filling the room. His muscles burned with power, longing to flex and unleash their power. But at the same time, Crow-Beast was light, lithe, and lightning-quick. A sharp beak and black eyes that saw perfectly in every light twitched and ticked in anticipation of the door opening.

"Well, we'll see what the night brings," the young janitor said in a thick accent and laughed as he flipped on the lights and entered the closet.

Crow-Beast Cain towered behind the young man, who was a big burly guy in his own right. Cain's purple-black claws flexed.

The janitor heard something first, then turned slowly. His mouth shook open. Tears sprang into his eyes. He whispered a plea to God in another language.

Crow-Beast's claws clamped around his arms, legs, and mouths. His wings wrapped around the janitor, encompassing him in darkness. Crow-Beast's wet black eyes came to the janitor's quivering ones. The only sound within the room was a ragged, wet breathing laid over the beeps and commotion of the hospital.

Cain began the spell, pouring his own essence, his own soul, from his Crow-Beast's eyes into the janitor's.

"What are you doing?" a sharp voice accused.

The door had never closed behind the janitor.

Someone was there. Cain was caught.

Chapter 14

Ivy

"**C**areful, clumsy dolt!" he barked feebly at Ivy, his breath curling up into a thick cloud, then dissipating into nothing.

Ivy bit her tongue as she tightened the electric blankets wrapped around each of his delicate, thin legs.

Soon.

Soon it would be all over, and she'd never have to put up with another hateful word from Grandpa again.

How had he become like this, ordering her around like a king's subject, muttering hurtful things, like she couldn't hear? Again, she told herself it was just the pressure. Grandpa was facing Death in the most literal sense and only had one chance at getting a lifetime's worth of planning right.

He muttered pagan prayers to himself, or maybe it was a list of Death's many names. Those alternated these days, but his eyes darted through the night air, searching fearfully and seemingly seeing things. It was impossible to fully understand what he was saying or what exactly he was even seeing. It was impossible to fully understand him.

But soon she would.

Maybe that was what Ivy wanted out of this more than anything else. Not the power or the taste of immortality but understanding. Connection. She wouldn't be alone anymore. She would never be alone again.

He seemed even more frail outside than in the sickly light of the room. His skin, like sheets drawn over broomsticks to make blanket forts, was sickly-colored and textured like ash as if a single touch would send his entire body crumbling to dust.

Was this the man who'd saved her from her father? The kind eyes and rough voice that told her stories about Ivanhoe, King Arthur, Thor, and Odysseus? The man who had pulled back the curtain of reality for Ivy, exposed the gears, taught her about the machinery of her reality and how it worked.

He'd trusted her, and her alone, with his life's work, the magnum opus of an occult scholar. It was amazing. She was chosen. She was seen. And the gift for being herself and following this great man was immortality.

Soon.

She squeezed the phone into her grandfather's hand and placed it back under the blanket. A burner phone from a convenience store with her number programmed into it and already dialed up. All he had to do was hit the green send button. Hopefully, if he needed her, if things went wrong, he could manage that.

"I'm going back inside, Grandpa."

MaKayla

She couldn't believe it. Just when Cain's forms couldn't get any more monstrous or weirder, here he was, some giant eight-foot-tall were-raven hypnotizing a poor custodian with what looked like magical black tears.

She shut the janitor closet door behind her with a click and a beep. "What are you doing?!" she whispered fiercely.

"Caah!" The glottal threat, more avian than human, was way too loud. They were definitely getting caught before they got anywhere near this assignment of Cain's.

"Shut up," she whispered, a shushing finger to her lips as she listened for noise at the door. Somehow, none came.

Cain morphed back into his human form, hand clamped snugly over the janitor's mouth. The man struggled against a captor whose appearance was suddenly much easier to process. The janitor thrashed to break free, screamed a muffled shout, and bulged his reddened, teary eyes almost all the way out.

Was this how she looked while gazing upon the scarier forms of Cain Morrigan?

Then Cain pulled the janitor in closer and planted a tiny kiss on the janitor's temple.

Immediately, the janitor's eyes rolled back, and he fell limp.

"What are you doing?" MaKayla asked for the third time.

"I'm utilizing his vessel to complete my assignment!"

"'Utilizing his vessel?' Are you going to *possess* this poor guy?"

"Of course not. Possession is from a ghost or demon. Now, MaKayla, you need to get out of here before things get danger-ous."

"Dangerous?" MaKayla couldn't take this. Her anxiety cup was already spilling over, and now, Cain had reached a new level of ridiculousness. "More dangerous than turning into a were-raven?"

"A were-raven?"

"Like a werewolf but a raven."

"I was a Crow-Beast, MaKayla, and yes, there are things more dangerous than a Crow-Beast. Please leave."

"I'm not going to let you possess this poor man. It's morally disgusting to remove his bodily autonomy like that."

"What, you want me to ask for his consent?"

"No, I want you to talk to me, Cain. Tell me what's actually going on here, so you and I can figure out how to complete your assignment without being a complete creep."

"And why would you help me, MaKayla? Why, after the way I treated you?"

"This has nothing to do with you, Cain. Nothing to do with you and me, anyway. If you missing an assignment is going to screw up all of reality, then I'm helping."

He was quiet for a minute.

"MaKayla, I do really owe you such an apology..."

"Shut. Up. We're here now. Let's focus. Your assignment is Ivy Skelton's grandfather. What else do I need to know?"

"How'd you find that out?"

"Trust me, I've learned a lot about Ivy Skelton. What else?"

"Well, it's her grandfather's connection, a heartstring, to Ivy that's making his soul difficult to cull. I need you to sever that heartstring before I can harvest his life."

"Is that his room at the top corner of the building?"

"Yep," Cain said. "You saw the giant gold ropes draping down out of the clouds?"

"I don't know what you saw, but those drooping masses were enormous clusters of woven lines. Not a big rope. A web."

"That could be Grandpa Skelton's occult connections to the

beyond. Maybe a secret society or two."

"Well, supposing we can both get by those webs," MaKayla thought aloud, "we still have to get Ivy out of the room. There's no way I could sneak in there and snip their loveline without getting found out."

"Perfect. We just have to get her out of his hospital room. Once there's a bit of distance, you can snip the connection in the hallway, and I can slip into the room as a shadow and harvest him."

"We also have to get up to the fourth floor without being seen."

"Yes."

"And figure out something to do with this poor guy."

The janitor appeared pretty at peace, snoring in the corner.

"He is currently under my dark control—"

"Bodily. Autonomy."

"I can awaken him in a few minutes. He'll have no recollection of the Crow-Beast."

After MaKayla's reluctant nod of approval, Cain set to work, whispering incantations into the passed-out janitor's ear.

Cain stood, giving MaKayla sorrowful eyes. God, was he going to apologize again?

"Thank you for coming back, MaKayla."

She ignored him. "Regroup at the vending machine room on the fourth floor; they're at the same place on every level. I'll handle Ivy."

"Wait," he said, grabbing her by the arm. The contact brought up feelings and a physical reaction. That her body betrayed her was so annoying.

She pulled away from him.

"How will you get up to the fourth floor? Are there nurse

scrubs in here to wear? Do you want his clothes?"

"That's stupid movie stuff. Never works. I'll just walk with purpose, and no one will bother me. And stop offering to do things without this guy's consent."

"Good luck, MaKayla. Be careful. If something happened to you, I'd never—"

"Shut. Up." MaKayla slipped out of the door, back into the noise of the hospital. "I miss the Crow-Beast."

Cain

His shadow filled the corners of the alcove, darkening the walls behind the vending machines. There were fewer people up on this floor, but it was louder. The closer to Death someone was, the louder Cain heard their medical apparatus. This night was a cacophony. The veil was thin.

Waiting was difficult, even knowing how much longer the trip up would take on foot.

Then, over the beeps, the hiss of oxygen tanks, and the rhythm of belabored breathing, footsteps. Tapping on the tile, echoing slightly.

MaKayla's footsteps.

"Miss?" a voice from somewhere.

The tapping of footsteps continued.

"Miss," the voice said more assertively.

The footsteps stopped.

The shadow that was Cain crept closer toward the voices in the hall.

After a big, wet sniffle, MaKayla said, "Yes?"

"What are you doing here, Miss?"

"It's my friend; I'm visiting him." Her voice was hoarse, rough and tired after the week he'd put her through. And now she was caught out in the open. Another thing that was his fault. She stuttered through crying, "We're friends from elementary school. We're gonna start a social media company together if he survives the cancer treatment ..."

She was laying it on thick, but maybe the nurse out there didn't want to hear it either.

"That's not one of *our* patients..." The words came out accusingly.

"Oh, he's not on this floor..." MaKayla was faltering, grasping. Cain prepared to swoop in.

"...But the vending machines there were out of caffeine-free mineral water."

This was bad.

The shadow that was Cain slid across the hall floor, causing some overhead lighting to flicker along his way until he was safe under the desk at the nurse's station.

"What is the patient's name, Miss?"

Cain's shadow pooled underneath the nurse interrogating MaKayla.

"I only know him as The Slice." She was so bad at lying.

"The Slice?" The nurse asked incredulously. Cain's shadow wrapped around her leg.

"That's what everybody calls him." MaKayla forced a chuckle.

"I'm calling security." The nurse picked the phone up. Cain could feel her pulse quicken. He was so close to an artery.

"No, don't," MaKayla pleaded.

"Young lady, what are you doing up here?" the nurse asked her again. Cain could stop her right there. Just take her life too.

But tonight wasn't going to be any more messy than it had to be.

"I'm sorry. I suck at lying. I'm worried about a girl I know, Ivy. Her grandad's here, and he's into weird stuff and may be like super abusive to her."

It was quiet. Cain was ready to strike.

There was a deep sigh. The nurse's heart rate slowed. "The Skelton girl?" she asked.

Another pause. Cain felt the nurse's pulse against his shade. She continued, "It's an odd family. She's here all the time."

"And her grandad's a little creepy, right?"

One more pause.

"Miss, I better not see or hear anything about you causing any trouble here. Do you know the room?"

"Far corner. Just going to get some snacks." The tapping of shoes started up again as MaKayla scurried by, back toward the vending machines.

Cain as a shadow slunk back to the floor, releasing the unknowing nurse. He slid back across the hall, the lights above flickering to darkness.

"What's that?" the nurse asked in his direction.

But he was already in the vending machine alcove. MaKayla was shaking out her arms and rubbing her face in her hands as if she were about to lose her sanity.

"Are you okay?" Cain checked in as he reformed into his human self.

"Man, I am no good at lying. I don't even know what I'm doing! I have no business trying to protect some cosmic balance of life and death! I'm a sophomore! I don't know if I'm here from some perverted sense of duty you or Mom gave me or if I'm just...helping you."

"MaKayla, you were great out there. You're great. I—"

"Cain, not again. No more apologies tonight. I can't handle it."

"I'm falling in love with you, MaKayla."

"No. No, you don't." She stuck a finger in his face like a loaded gun. "Just because I don't want to watch you fail and die doesn't mean you get to take my feelings and run with them. Live through tonight before you lay on any more of your BS. I don't have the time or bandwidth for it right now."

"Okay. Sorry."

"And no more apologies."

"Okay. So how do we distract—"

Just then, a door clicked open around the corner from them.

"No, I'm with Grandpa." Ivy Skelton's voice was hushed and hurried as she stepped out of the room. Immediately, footsteps gave away which hall she went down. "He's...not great." A door whined open. Her squeaky footsteps took her further away. "It's only a matter of time."

She sounded upset, but not at the news of Grandpa. Ivy didn't seem to get worried; she worried other people. Something upsetting her had to be a pretty big deal.

But Cain pushed that out of his mind. Ivy was out of the room. The plan was working. MaKayla's distraction worked.

They were doing this.

Cain whispered, "Follow her and cut the connection. I'll give you a two-minute head start, then head into the room."

But this time, there was no snarky comeback from MaKayla. She understood, too, that this was the endgame. It was either going to work or not. Either way, they had to try.

She took a deep breath, eyes closed and head down. When she looked back up, her face was set in stone, her eyes steady as carved rock.

Without another word, she marched back into the hallway, around the corner, tapping footsteps along the tiles until that same door whined open and closed once again.

The darkness that was Cain Morrigan slid along the floor, through wall after wall, phasing from a muffled room to a loud hall to the silence of Grandpa Skelton's hospital room.

The room was dark, all of the shades pulled, including a privacy ring around the bed. Cain didn't risk changing forms until the last moment. Until then, he had to assume MaKayla was able to cut the thread.

Cain's shadow crept along tiles, over Ivy's backpack on the floor, and finally, under the curtain.

There was no turning back now. His mind raced. Every lesson, reminder, and criticism from his father flashed through his mind.

He pooled his darkness at the edge of the hospital bed. From his shadow, his hand emerged, then his arm. He rose from the shadow on the floor. His black-nailed finger and thumb pinched the hospital blanket. MaKayla must have cut the heartstring by now.

He couldn't screw this up. He couldn't fail; too much was at stake. Cain had to get this right.

His arm tensed.

He threw back the sheet.

The bed was empty.

MaKayla

She paused before opening the door. MaKayla had definitely

seen Ivy head up these stairs, but the loveline was nowhere to be seen. She wouldn't be able to get to it from here.

She could either risk getting caught following Ivy out onto the roof, or risk blowing Cain's cover by going back to Grandpa Skelton's room. Neither was a great choice but screwing up Cain's mission also screwed up the overall mission.

Maybe this could be a good thing? A chance to talk to Ivy about what she was doing. Maybe even a chance to counsel someone through the severing of a heartstring.

So she zipped up her short tight puffy coat, unsheathed her shears, and pushed one of the two big double doors open.

The icy wind blew in her face while thick flakes of snow drifted eerily slowly down. Outside was so quiet, the foot and a half of snow dampening and absorbing any sound. Coming from the beeps, footsteps, voices, and announcements from the hospital interior, the silence was shocking.

MaKayla took a deep breath, clutched her shears, and stepped onto the wet salted roof of the hospital. She didn't see Ivy until it was too late.

When one gloved hand wrapped around her mouth, something struck MaKayla in the fingers. A hard, hot pain so sudden it was disorienting. MaKayla struggled against her captor, who grunted through a soothing whisper, "MaKayla, shh, it's alright. It'll all be over soon. It's all over. Just slow down."

MaKayla had no leverage from this position. Ivy locked her in from behind and knocked the shears out of her hand. MaKayla had no choice. She stopped struggling.

"Thank you. This will all be over soon."

MaKayla was released and immediately took a step away from Ivy, looking around on the wet, salty rooftop, searching for her shears. She felt that they were near but couldn't see them.

The feeling that they were so close but out of her possession was unnerving. Panic filled her as she realized she was utterly helpless, stuck on this rooftop with a superior fighter, without her shears or any form of defense.

"This should keep you quiet." Ivy held up a yellow-browned scrap of old parchment paper about the size of a postage stamp. On it, a symbol, maybe a letter in another language, burned brightly. Soon the scrap of paper burned up to a flame consuming it into ash and smoke, then the letter and paper were gone.

MaKayla was about to laugh off the party magician's trick, maybe get a snide dig on Ivy and a little illusion that must've been super impressive to kids...but when MaKayla opened her mouth to speak, she couldn't. An invisible grip squeezed her throat, allowing enough room to breathe but tightened when MaKayla attempted to speak. The words squished into nothing before she could say anything.

"This will all be over soon, Colfax." Ivy removed her knit gloves and began slipping on a series of mismatched rings. MaKayla attempted to scream again, and Ivy just shook her head without looking up from the jewelry she carefully aligned on her fingers. "Stop fighting. Change is hard."

MaKayla silently screamed as Ivy bound her wrists.

Cain

He searched wildly, under the bed, the small closet, the little bathroom. The old man was nowhere to be found. Cain's assignment was on the move.

What was worse was that Cain couldn't sense the old man's

presence. Before, in human form, he'd always been able to tell where an assignment was, at least which cardinal direction. But not now. It was as if Grandpa Skelton had vanished or someone else had done the job of ending him.

While gripping the bar on the side of the bed to check behind it, Cain felt it, something rough carved into the plastic. A symbol, some ancient tune, most likely pagan, but not one that Cain recognized.

Then next to it, another, and another. Runes scrawled on the little plastic gate that surrounded the bed, but also in the rubber lip of the tray for the bed. And the wall behind, and the stand for his IV, the rolling desk for his heart monitor. Little runes everywhere.

In the arms of the chairs beside the bed, above the vents of the air conditioning, in the paint of the window frame, runes, ancient symbols of mystical power, all spaced out, all unrecognizable to Cain. They were preventing him from sensing Grandpa Skelton.

Something was wrong. Something serious. He pulled his phone out and called MaKayla.

"Cain Morrigan," answered a voice which was not MaKayla's. "A nice guy in bad trouble. It's time to come get your trouble."

"Ivy."

Whatever Ivy Skelton was playing at, Cain had no idea. He should have questioned MaKayla earlier when she said she learned things about Ivy. There was a serious possibility that Ivy had been paying MaKayla and Cain all week, somehow knowing their secrets, maybe going so far as manipulating Mark and Aurora.

Ivy went on, "And I'm not alone. But you better come alone, Cain Morrigan. I'll see you on the roof."

MaKayla

To Hell with Cain Morrigan. MaKayla was over it. Here she was, suspended five stories up over the side of the building, the fragile framework of life and death hanging in the balance, all because Cain Morrigan was too scared to ask his dad for help.

If she ever got out of this, she'd kill him. Worse, she'd embarrass him in front of the entire school. She'd tell his parents on him. She'd tell him what she really thought of him.

Every aspect of her life had been made worse by Cain this week. Just trying to get her shears back might have split up her parents. Severing her first connection set off a drug deal parking lot brawl. And she'd barely learned more from Cain and his half-assed perusal of an ancient mystic library than she had from a simple internet search.

Both doors to the roof swung out, Cain landing on the wet rooftop clumsily landing from his kick. Why on Earth didn't he just walk out? He probably thought he looked cooler than he did. Because he looked stupid. When he gained his feet and the clouded flurry of snow had resumed its slow drift, he seemed nervous. Eyes wild, desperate. He was hunched, hands at the ready.

MaKayla opened her mouth to scream out for him, but no sound came. Floating within Ivy's enchantment, she hovered a few feet above the roof, no way to run to him, nothing to kick or jump from to get his attention. As Cain stepped further out on the rooftop, MaKayla drifted back around the corner where he couldn't see.

She had no idea where Ivy was by then.

Silently, she prayed that Cain would take the moment needed to scope the roof out, to maybe find her, maybe even figure out where Ivy went.

But instead, he headed for Grandpa Skelton, who sat in a folding chair in the middle of the H of the hospital's helicopter landing platform, wrapped in blankets, hair blowing wildly in the cold. Even MaKayla could see the grandad was bait. But it was too tempting for Cain.

A couple glances over his shoulders, then he scurried over to the old man. Cain's silhouette, black on black clothing against a gray sky and the ever-reaching white landscape frosting the edges of the hospital roof, blossomed. His figure bloomed, opened up like a flower of unfurling black cloth with white bone sprouting out until Cain the young man no longer stood, but instead, his enormous skeletal form stood, covered in patches of flowing black, dancing in the night wind.

He was monstrous, a mishmash of animal bones, a collage of skeletons. MaKayla couldn't stand how beautiful he seemed. And suddenly, she could see more — the giant drooping ropes reaching up from Grandpa Skelton into the snow clouds, the fiery bright golden heartstring reaching out from his chest but fading into a swirl of foreign symbols. She could see the weak light of the old man's aura. And for a moment, she thought she could almost sense the possible futures playing out before her.

Then the skeletal beast of Cain's Reaper form reached a humanoid hand toward the shivering old man. And she understood what the drooping ropes really were. But she could not warn Cain.

Suddenly, the blanketed old man lurched. His entire aura shrank, receding into a glow in his gut. Immediately, his papery pale skin faded to gray translucent. He slumped. The glowing light, what must have been a human soul, floated to Cain's boney hand.

The trap was tripped. The massive drooping ropes dropped. Heartstrings, netting, webbing, knots, and weaving tightened into a ball of light and color surrounding Cain's skeletal form. Encasing him.

He panicked, running into netting, kicking away so much his back legs tangled, and he fell. His fiery black eyes, slick within his horse-like horned skull, found MaKayla. Fear. Inhuman and immediate.

"Ye gods, it worked." Ivy sounded truly amazed, walking out onto the helipad and passing her grandfather's limp body to the ensnared monstrous Reaper. "You crazy old idiot, you were right. I'm going to live forever!"

Cain

"Cain? Cain, can you hear me? Are you still in there? I don't want to hurt you any more than I have to. I want to make this quick, you understand? But that all depends on you."

She paced around him, adjusting the multiple rings adorning her fingers.

The enormous skeletal Cain didn't look up at her but stayed down, cradling the grandfather's glowing soul.

Then he saw MaKayla, invisibly restrained and floating helplessly, and he lost it. He struggled and lashed against the magical bindings. His bones were greeted with searing burns and shocks of paralyzed limbs.

No, he couldn't let Ivy do this.

"Stop," he tried to say. But without lungs, vocal cords, or lips, the only sound he made was the clacking of dry bones. He was helpless, as was MaKayla; at the mercy of a maniacal classmate who had completely fooled him. He should have listened and stayed away. He should have done a lot of things.

That evil succubus Ivy stopped her cocky saunter right in Cain's line of vision, preventing him from seeing MaKayla dangling above the rooftop.

Ivy stooped down, and Cain pointed his bleached bone snout up at her. There was a sadness in her eyes, either her own or pity for Cain's predicament.

"I am going to change you back into a human, but before then, I need you to give me that." She gestured to the glowing orb of light Cain protected. She continued, slowly and gently, "And then I'll let her go."

Ivy pointed with the pair of shears over at their owner, MaKayla, still bound by invisible forces, who violently shook her head no. Her teary eyes pleaded with Cain. He knew he couldn't trust Ivy; the words of a witch, or a wizard, or whatever type of dark magic practitioner she was.

But he could never let anything happen to MaKayla. He could never hurt her again.

Still holding onto the soul, Cain extended a finger and pointed to MaKayla.

MaKayla shut her eyes and shook her head no. Always so stubborn. But he loved that about her.

Ivy fidgeted her fingers and whispered something under her breath. The spell released. MaKayla fell to the ground.

With another gesture of fingers, Ivy pointed to her grandfather's soul.

It floated out of Cain's grasp.

"Ivy!" MaKayla pleaded, yelling over whipping winds. "Ora says she misses you! She loves and misses you. She would text you, but she said you blocked her. I have texts from her right here." MaKayla dug into her pockets.

Whatever she was talking about, whatever was happening, Cain didn't understand and couldn't fight. Helpless. Everything was unraveling, and he couldn't move.

Ivy continued whispering her spell, the orb of light coming to touch her fingertip. She whispered a word.

Fire burst from nowhere, flames exploding out of Ivy's skin, blasting off pieces of her clothing, exposing dark magic runes on her skin, hissing out their evil power. Her eyes whitened with the light of the soul as her silhouette brightened and expanded. A halo, an aura, emanated around her, surrounding her. No, not an aura; a projection of a larger human form, the soul of Grandpa Skelton expanding. Two powerful souls overfilling one body.

"I was right!" a voice beyond Ivy poured out of her mouth. She agreed evenly, less cocky than before, down low with humanity. "Yes, Grandpa."

An arm made of solid light flung out to accuse Cain, who couldn't help but flinch. The uber-voice continued, "And now you, Lickspittle. You who cannot understand nor appreciate your own power shall surrender your powers of Death to me. For I am the true end of—"

Ivy's earthly scowl interrupted, "Enough. Begin the spell."

"Command me not, girl!"

Ivy continued reciting an incantation. The inflated voice joined. Cain couldn't make out the words. He was suddenly cold. Then the strength was ripped from him, dragged out from his gut; the blackness, the comforting lonely darkness, the cold inhumanity he tasted with every shift of form. His Reaper form, but also all the rest, gone.

It flowed like black water across the night, out of Cain, into the Ivy who was more than Ivy.

And then, he was nothing more than human.

MaKayla

MaKayla couldn't believe what she was seeing but understood it clearly. Possessed Ivy had stripped Cain of his Reaperness.

"And now to move along to your superior," the godlike voice boomed. "Something to get his attention."

With a wave of his ghost hand, Cain was flung aside, tossed like a rag-doll.

MaKayla's heart jumped. She had to run and save him. He was human; couldn't he die now?

No, she had to stick to the plan. Even if Possessed Ivy had MaKayla's shears, she wasn't completely helpless. All she had to do was buy time.

It took a lot to drag her eyes away from the bright, evil being that Ivy had become and pull up Ora's texts on her phone. But when it was up, she read off the paragraphs Ora had sent.

"'Lil Boo Bear, I miss you and your stinky pits.'"

For an instant, Possessed Ivy hesitated.

Cain pushed up from the ground, arms swimming through the snow piled on the roof's ledge.

MaKayla pushed on. "'Don't get me wrong, you know I love to get in there. I miss your stinky pits.'"

Possessed Ivy resumed, squaring up with Cain. MaKayla got as loud as she could, just spewing out the words of the text. "'I miss your warm boobs and cold hands. I miss the freckle by your eye. But I just miss talking. About nothing. About why aren't sandwich bags sold in a bigger sandwich bag?'"

Possessed Ivy waved a ghost hand again, and Cain was dragged to his feet, invisible power clutching him standing him on the ledge of the hospital roof. Possessed Ivy closed in on him, but he ignored her completely, locking eyes with MaKayla. Tears traced down his high cheek, plunging off his jaw, down his neck, to the flash of purple, an edge of the bandana MaKayla gave him. He wore it. A color. For her.

She screamed out the rest of the text, "'I miss the weird way you pronounce 'bagel.'"

Possessed Ivy hesitated again. This time, the godlike voice huffed in frustration, "Is this the nonsense with that Black girl again?"

Ivy spat back, "What do you mean, 'that Black girl?'"

The god voice groaned, swatting a ghost hand into the falling snow. Cain faltered. The plan wasn't working; MaKayla's plan was failing. One of Cain's feet slipped. His leg gave, and his slender figure toppled out toward the forever-reaching snowy night.

MaKayla gasped, her mind opened at what unraveled before her: the possibilities of a life without Cain. She could see herself growing into her powers, becoming strong, coming to terms with her lineage, reconciling with the past, and accepting herself as a superhuman being, a Fate. Then she saw a future in which she did all of that with Cain by her side. Yes, he'd complicate things, get under her skin, and distract her completely.

But it would be so much more fun.

There were things coming. Things she was destined for. Good and bad. Movement on the horizon. She could take on this future with or without Cain.

Then Mom appeared at the door. Mom made it, and this plan

could actually work. It had to. The plan had to work because she had to save Cain. She loved him. It was so obvious, as obvious as the shears that were now in her hand.

Holy shit, her shears were back in her hand.

Ahead, Cain fell away. Back off the ledge to go down, down right alongside the snow.

The heartstring between them grew taut. A loveline. It was bright and complex and filled with love. With her free hand, she wound it around the heartstring twice and tugged with all her might. The string pulled tight. Cain's foot caught on the ledge.

He hung there, leaning impossibly back, a wire leading from his heart, his toe barely staying on the ledge. They held onto each other. An intimate moment from across the roof.

Ivy

This wasn't how this was supposed to be. Ivy was supposed to have more control than this. This was supposed to be a partnership, but in reality, she was a puppet.

Meanwhile, right in front of her, the nice guy from Algebra 2, the guy she and her grandfather were killing for his powers, was literally hanging by an invisible thread.

Ivy had never seen any magic like whatever was connecting MaKayla and Cain. She *caught* him. They were saving each other. Grandpa would have to summon a god of Death with some other victim.

And nobody would come to save Ivy.

"Mom, cut the red wire!" MaKayla called out. Honestly, Ivy was just relieved the girl stopped reading texts from Ora. What had Grandpa called her, 'that Black girl'? No, Ivy couldn't think about that. Grandpa was right. They had to summon a Death god. Grandpa was right; they could do this. They could defeat Death. They could live forever.

But then some woman came rushing from the hospital. Was this MaKayla's mom? A mortal? Here to do what exactly?

Running back toward Grandpa's snow-collecting body, the woman brandished scissors of her own. What was it with this family and scissors? She looked down at the weapon she'd confiscated from MaKayla, but it was gone.

The woman reached out into the night, splitting the distance between Ivy and Grandpa's body, and snipped at the air.

Furious, Grandpa swatted at her, sending the old lady flying off.

Ivy felt relief, then release.

What was it that old lady snipped? Why did Ivy suddenly feel differently? Why was she suddenly thinking differently? She realized she didn't want to live forever. She liked learning how; she loved learning all of the ancient ways, the forgotten secrets between humanity and the heavens, but she didn't crave immortality. Not like Grandpa. He wanted the powers of Death for all of time.

Grandpa. The liar, the poisonous bully who emotionally abused her until she was pliable enough to make into a vessel. *His* vessel.

All the moments she didn't speak, each insult she laughed off, every sexist wish for a grandson she deflected, every bit of poison he fed her in the name of family and success, every one of them now stood plainly in her mind. He'd used her. For years.

She owed him nothing, least of all herself. She was free. She was no longer bound to his will. No longer tied to him.

So she let him go. The bright light that was lifting her up vanished, her boots crunching on the roof. And Grandpa evaporated away. Crossed over.

Ivy was back. It was her, only her, doing only what *she* wanted. She ran over and helped MaKayla pull Cain back onto the roof.

Cain

The power flowed back into Cain as he regained footing. MaKayla rushed into his arms.

She'd done it. She saved him. She saved everything. That old man was usurping the throne of Death and would have gained power over the realm of man, and MaKayla Colfax and her mom stopped him.

Cain would never underestimate her ever again.

His fingers searched through her dark hair freckled with snowflakes, finding her face. His lips met hers, and the night's magic rushed up to meet them, to fill them, to celebrate their victory alongside them.

But then a shadow descended. A chill passed by, flickering lights and disturbing the natural fall of snow. There was someone else here now, something else. Cain recognized the presence immediately. Father.

There was no running or hiding. No lying to get out of this one. He'd screwed up. Bad. Thanks to his own stubbornness, Cain could have ruined the balance of life and death for all eternity. He could have even caused the end of all things himself.

Cain released MaKayla and stood to face the giant specter of his father, an oversized yellowing skeleton enrobed in a black hooded robe, towering over them all.

"Father, I'm so sorry—"

"I'm not here for you," the recognizable voice growled with annoyance but wet with sadness, regret.

"You're not?"

"I'm here for her." Dad's enormous Reaper form floated over toward the opposite edge of the roof, where Mrs. Colfax lay crumpled, propped against the roof ledge.

MaKayla

"No," MaKayla's voice choked with begging.

"It's you." Mom sounded so tired, head lolling to see the giant Grim Reaper looking over them.

"It's me," the kind voice of Cain's father emanated from within the rippling black hood.

Mom wheezed out words with her breath. "I always thought I could beat you."

"Many think that."

"Will she be okay?" Mom gestured weakly to MaKayla.

Death, or Mr. Morrigan, shrugged, then vanished.

Mom locked eyes with MaKayla until she didn't. Mom slumped, and her focus fell slack. MaKayla fell to her knees and wept, all of reality vibrating, humming, buzzing, screaming around her.

It wasn't fair. It wasn't right that the world was allowed to continue as if nothing had changed. It was wrong of reality to ignore the monumental shift that occurred. But everything kept on, moving impossibly fast. The world buzzed along. Life continued.

Her only constant was Cain's arms clutching her, holding her down so she didn't vibrate away into the chaos. The world moved in fast motion as first responders showed up, a parade of brightly colored clothes lit by flashes and strobes, all moving faster than MaKayla followed. Everything was too fast now. Reality was off. Mom was dead. And nothing would ever be right again.

Two weeks later

Aurora

The slow-motion falling of the snow aggravated her to no end. Winter was melancholy enough, but it was the beginning of May, and a chill that saddened Aurora to her bones was still around. On top of that, the eerie vacancy of a school on the weekend creeped her out.

It was different when she was cheering, surrounded by friends, drunk with the reckless sensation of existing in a space at a forbidden time. Then, the whole school was a playground: desks, tables, chairs, and counters were scaled, climbed, stood, and lounged upon.

But now, with a week left of school, this was the last place any student would be. Which was perfect for someone trying to avoid every other student.

MaKayla Colfax and Aurora had been friends since the third grade, ever since MaKayla wrapped half of her cookie in a torn-out comic book page to give Aurora on a tough first day. And she'd been there pretty much every day since, even when MaKayla wasn't allowed to have sleepovers or camp with scouts, and that was all Aurora lived for. Even when Aurora got so depressed about her ex-boyfriend Mark's drinking that she absolutely unloaded on MaKayla for no discernible reason.

And through it all, MaKayla was still there to talk trash at the art store where they both worked, still there to text or talk and vent, still there with a little nonsense gift elaborately presented when Aurora needed it most.

But everything changed two weeks ago. MaKayla and her new friend (sounded complicated) Cain drove by and snuck an exhausted Ivy Skelton up to Aurora's bedroom. Ivy and Aurora had a complicated relationship. They'd been fast friends, too. And then they were friends with secrets from the world, then secrets from each other, then after so much, they became strangers again.

Aurora was happy to have Ivy back in her life, even though they taking it slow, barely texting once a day so far.

But she missed MaKayla. She basically became a recluse after she lost her mother.

And what on Earth could Aurora do to help someone in that situation?

Parking by the old loading dock that was now the school's art studio, Aurora knew she was about to find out. She parked her new SUV next to MaKayla's hand-me-down coupe. One garage door cracked half open, like the sleepy school building was yawning.

Inside the art studio, it took a minute for Aurora's eyes to adjust. A black figure stood alone in the expansive room. Blooming balls of fire erupted around the darkened person, pointing and shooting fire as they pleased. The sight was surreal and terrifying until Aurora realized it was someone using a blowtorch in full-body safety equipment.

The figure pushed up a welder's mask to reveal MaKayla's face, smiling and smudged with soot. "Hi."

"Hi, I brought you lunch." Aurora dropped a bag of burgers from a local diner and dug in.

MaKayla removed her comically oversized gloves and jacket, still wearing big puffy fireproof pants with a hot pink tank top.

MaKayla must have been working in the heat for a while as her whole body steamed in the cool air.

"How close to finished are you?" Aurora asked because MaKayla loved talking about her art.

"Well…" MaKayla lifted up a series of burnt panels, sliding them into place on a vertical frame. "I'm actually pretty much done."

It was a foldable screen with a scene on it in collage. A young girl in a colorful pink and purple bedroom looked into the mirror. She was literally made up of rainbows and kittens, small printed-out images forming her smiling face and rosy cheeks. In the mirror, an older version of the girl looked back, melancholy. This face was made of photos of big cats, giant hunting felines cut out among rain clouds. But Aurora's eye was drawn to the room in the reflection. The older girl's room was a mirror copy of the purple and pink one, only it was burned. Charred and crispy edges of wallpaper framed burnt family photos, all faces in the photos smudged or torn.

The entire art piece was breathtaking, even if Aurora didn't understand it.

Makayla sat down, happily divvying up the food while Aurora took it all in.

"How's school?" MaKayla asked.

"Tragic," Aurora said, joining her. "Begging to get back into cheerleading and all the clubs and classes I quit. How's your dad and brother doing?"

MaKayla shrugged, then said with her mouth full, "As good as can be expected. There's a lot of legal paperwork Dad has to deal with."

"How are you and Cain?"

That brought a smile to MaKayla's face. "Good. He's officially my boyfriend."

"Ooooh!" Aurora nudged her friend playfully.

This was so great. MaKayla was a wonderful person and deserved to be happy. Aurora always hated that her bestie had never managed a boyfriend until now.

"Yeah, I think we make each other pretty happy. I think...he's made losing Mom a lot easier. How are you and Ivy?"

"Like walking on eggshells. We're just staying friends for now. She has a lot of mental shuffling to do. So I'm just off to the side if she needs me."

"That's good. You're a good friend, Ora. She'll need that."

"Thanks." They both peeled back greasy paper and ate in silence for a moment. But Aurora had something to say, and if she didn't speak up then, she'd wind up leaving without saying her peace. "So...I talked to Mark."

"Okay. How was that for you?"

"It's really fine. I've never had a break-up like this, like all of my feelings, all of the emotions I had tied to him just up and vanished. We're both, like, totally over each other and have managed to be friends. Like, real friends."

"Well, that's good."

"Yeah. Well. You know I said he used to have, like, these visions that we were meant to be together?"

"Yeah. Creepy."

"Yeah, part of me looks back at those as huge red flags, but...

Mark keeps having these visions. Only not about me."

"Like what?"

"Well, I don't want to upset you, but he had a vision...right after we broke up, a day before you and Cain dropped off Ivy at my place...and I don't want to upset you, but he had a vision of you at the hospital, on the roof, holding Cain up by a rope."

MaKayla stopped chewing. Her face blanched. "He had that vision the day *before* we dropped Ivy off at your place?"

"Yeah. And he had another vision with you in it. He asked me to tell you. To warn you. I told him he was being silly, creepy like you said—"

"No, no. Ora, tell me."

"He says a woman is coming for you. A woman with scissors. But Mark said to warn you, she's only bringing you lies. Lies and death. And if you believe her, if you trust her, you will die."

THE END

Reader, if you enjoyed this story, please help it find more readers! If you thought it was any good, please tell your friends. Recommend it for your book club! Give it as a gift! Shout it from the rooftops! And if you don't have any rooftops handy, PLEASE post about this book on social media. Thank you again for your time and brainpower reading.

Want to know how Cain Morrigan found out he was a Grim Reaper? And how he got so grumpy? Sign up at JeffriesBooks.com and read the prequel novella, Angel of Brimstone!

-z